WHISKEY LULLABY

An Addison Holmes Novel

LILIANA HART

DEDICATION

To Scott -

Thank you for taking me on trips and buying me snacks when I'm stuck in a story. You understand my process well. And thanks for loving me when I want to throw every book in the trash and start over at the halfway point. You're an awesome husband.

ALSO BY LILIANA HART

The Scarlet Chronicles

Bouncing Betty

Hand Grenade Helen

Front Line Francis

The Harley and Davidson Mystery Series

The Farmer's Slaughter

A Tisket a Casket

I Saw Mommy Killing Santa Claus

Get Your Murder Running

Deceased and Desist

Malice in Wonderland

Tequila Mockingbird

Gone With the Sin

Grime and Punishment

Blazing Rattles

A Salt and Battery

Curl Up and Dye

First Comes Death Then Comes Marriage

Box Set 1

Box Set 2

Box Set 3

The Gravediggers

The Darkest Corner

Gone to Dust

Say No More

PROLOGUE

They say it's not over till the fat lady sings.

I wasn't fat yet, but my time was coming. I figured it was best to get my last rodeo out of the way before cankles and stretch marks set in. Though technically, my last rodeo had been a few weeks ago when I'd closed my last case. But retirement had caused a proverbial hitch in my get-along.

I wasn't sure where all the cowboy imagery was coming from, but I'd been having weird dreams that Sam Elliott was trying to recruit me to become a US Marshal and hunt down outlaws. Sam also wanted me to put a bit in his mouth and ride him like a stallion, but I declined because I'm a married woman now.

Pregnancy hormones are weird.

My name is Addison Holmes, and I'm no stranger to weird. It was a miracle Nick had married me at all. I'm Southern by birth, which means I come from a long line of crazy. The good news is Nick is Southern too, so he wouldn't know what to do with a normal woman.

My mother always said that good intentions paved the road to hell, and my intention had been to retire from the PI world and move on to the next phase of my life. I had no idea what that phase was going to be. I was in what the experts liked to call "transition." The limbo of not knowing anything about my future, except that there'd be a tiny human attached to it, was daunting to say the least, and I'll be the first to admit I wasn't handling it all that well.

Between Sam Elliott and my murky future, it didn't take a psychologist to know that I was missing the action my previous life provided. I was the kind of woman who needed adventure and excitement. In truth, I'd become an adrenaline junky and I didn't know what to do with myself. Which might have been the reason I'd agreed to take this case, even though I'd told Nick I was done with PI work forever. Which was why this was going to be my little secret.

For the past couple of years, I've been halfway decent at my job at the McClean Detective Agency. I was as surprised as anyone else as far as the halfway decent moniker went. It's not skill or experience I possess, so much as bulldog tenacity and luck.

Sometimes my tenacity got me into trouble. I could have turned this whole thing over to a veteran

PI, the cops, or even the FBI. But this case hit close to home, and I'd promised my mother I'd take care of it without dragging our family name through the mud. But considering Aunt Scarlet had been dragging our name through the mud for years, I wasn't so sure what she was worried about. Holmes women had been making headlines for decades.

I was pretty sure if I got out of this alive I'd be making more than headlines, because if Nick became aware of my current situation I'd have to move to another country.

Vince Walker was my stepfather, and I'd tracked him to a fishing cabin on the bayou where I'd hoped to catch him in the throes of passion with a twenty-something townie skank.

I'd been there about five minutes when a car had pulled up and Vince had shushed me and shoved me out the back door onto a floating dock the size of a doormat that moved every time I shifted my weight. He told me to avoid the flotants and keep quiet.

I didn't know what a flotant was, and if I'd had cell service I would've Googled it, but I figured whatever it was, I'd at least be able to see it coming for me. There was a pirogue tied to the dock and it swayed gently in the marshy green water. Gnats and other bugs hovered over the scummy surface, and other things I didn't want to think about made creaking noises off into the mossy trees.

The bayou was a cacophony of smells—hot mud, dirty dishwater, and fish—for the most part. My sense of smell had become heightened over the past few weeks—meaning if the wind blew the wrong way I was probably going to throw up. I was going to have to add the bayou to the growing list of things that made me vomit, along with pancake batter, air freshener, and concrete after it rained. Like I said, pregnancy is weird.

The temperature was a lot colder on the water, and I shivered in my brand-new leather jacket, wishing I'd gone for practicality instead of style. But there was no use crying over spilled milk, and at least I looked really good while I shivered uncontrollably.

I wasn't sure who'd driven up, and Vince hadn't said, but he had mentioned there were only a couple of people he could trust with the information he'd found out. Considering the delicate nature of said information, I hoped he knew what he was doing.

I decided standing on a swaying dock wasn't in my best interest, and I couldn't see or hear anything from my current position. I was one of those people who had constant FOMO—fear of missing out—and I needed to see what was happening in the worst way.

My choices were limited. I tried to recall the layout of the fishing cabin, at least what I'd seen of it. It was basically one main room that served as a bedroom and living room, a small kitchen that was no more than a sink, a microwave, and a minifridge, and a closed door I could only assume was the bathroom.

My best chance of curing my FOMO was to make my way over to the kitchen side where there were two small windows. I leaned as far as I could without toppling into the water to see what the layout was like.

There were stilts spaced evenly apart on the entire left side of the cabin, as if someone had planned to build onto the structure at some point. They stuck up about two feet out of the water, and if I could manage to stand on one I'd be able to look into the window.

I was feeling pretty optimistic about my chances of success. The mucky water surrounded almost the entire house, but there seemed to be solid ground just on the other side of the kitchen window, leading back up to the front.

I debated whether or not to untie the pirogue and row myself to my destination, but I was afraid it'd make too much noise if I accidentally hit one of the stilts. I wasn't exactly Sir Francis Drake when it came to boats. My only other option was to jump from stilt to stilt until I reached the window.

I heard a car door slam and knew my time was limited to get into place without being seen or heard, so I took a deep breath and channeled my inner ninja warrior. The stilts were a good size, big enough I could fit both feet on them, but there wasn't extra room for forgiveness if I missed my target.

I wiped sweaty palms on my jeans, said a little prayer, and then stepped onto the first stilt, which just happened to be directly beside the dock. It was solid beneath my feet, and I let out a *whoosh* of surprise. I didn't give myself time to think or I would've chickened out. I jumped to the next one. And then the next. Until finally I stood on the one just outside the kitchen window.

I had to admit it felt good to know that marriage and pregnancy hadn't totally stolen my mojo.

If I stood on my tiptoes I could barely see in the kitchen window. I gasped in surprise as I saw Vince staring back at me, his lips thin and his eyes narrowed. I was used to this look from men, so I gave him a thumbs-up, and he blew out a breath and went to answer the knock at the door

Vince stood with his back to me and his weapon drawn and down at his side while he cracked the door an inch to see who it was. Then he opened it wider and let two men inside.

They were older, probably in their late fifties to early sixties, and I could tell by looking at them they were cops. Or at least they used to be. Cops all looked the same—not in physical appearance, but there was something in the eyes that was a dead giveaway. My father had the same look.

I didn't recognize either of the men, but Vince shifted where he stood so when they faced him they didn't have a clear shot of the kitchen window. Vince put his weapon back in the holster.

"Jimmy," Vince said, shaking the man's hand.

Jimmy was tall and lean, and he seemed to be in

good shape despite his age, and he was very hand-some. His hair was thick and silver, and his face clean shaven, showing a little dimple at the chin.

"Bruce," Vince said, reaching out to the other man. Bruce was considerably shorter than Jimmy, maybe a couple of inches taller than my own five foot eight. His hair was dark and thinning on top, but his mustache was *Super Mario Brothers* quality. He was also quite a bit thicker through the middle than his friend. They both wore khakis and loose button-down shirts that screamed retirement.

"Thanks for coming," Vince told them.

"Anything for you, Vince," Bruce said, clapping Vince on the back. "It's not like we've got anything better to do. Retirement isn't all it's cracked up to be." I raised my brows at that tidbit. I'd called that one right. "I've remodeled every room in our house, and Helen told me if I didn't get out of her hair she was going to put me in a home. Thirty years of marriage, and the woman wants to put me in a home."

Vince snorted out a laugh and seemed to relax some. "Could be worse. She could want you dead. Cop wives are very resourceful. Remember back when Johnny Russo kept getting those stomach aches and no one could figure out what was wrong with him? I swear his wife was poisoning him."

"Well," Bruce said. "Johnny Russo was a horse's ass. Who could blame her?"

"I heard he died in a car crash a few years ago," Vince said.

"May he rest in peace," Bruce said, giving the sign of the cross and then spitting on the floor. "Probably drunk, the worthless bastard."

Jimmy slapped Vince on the back a couple of times, his smile wide. "It's been too long, Vinny. It's like you disappeared after you retired. How come you don't come to none of the get-togethers with the old crew? Too good for us?"

"Nah," Vince said, hands on hips. "I just discovered there's more to life after retirement. I don't want to sit around and drink beer and talk about the good old days. I moved to Whiskey Bayou and started over. Now I get to travel and do all the things I never got a chance to do when I was on the job."

"I heard you started your new life with Charlie Holmes's wife," Bruce said, waggling his eyebrows. "How come you didn't send us invitations to the wedding? More than twenty years we worked together and you can't spare some wedding cake?"

"You were always first in line for cake," Vince said.

Bruce put his hands on his round stomach. "Yeah, but now my metabolism is shot, and Helen has me eating celery sticks and gluten-free everything."

"Doesn't seem to be working," Jimmy said.

Bruce gave a boisterous laugh. "That's 'cause she don't know about my secret stash."

"She only wants you to think that," Jimmy said. "Wives know everything."

Bruce pursed his lips. "Says the guy that's been divorced three times."

Jimmy rolled his eyes. "I've been divorced three times because wives know everything."

Vince shook his head, his smile wide. It was clear these men were his friends, and he enjoyed their company. I couldn't figure out why I was standing on a stilt in the swamp and not inside where the floor heater was going full blast.

"In this case you didn't miss out on any cake," Vince told them. "Phyllis and I got married by Elvis in one of the little chapels in Vegas. We said our vows and they gave us buffet vouchers and a bottle of champagne."

"That's the smart way to do it," Bruce said, nodding his head in agreement. "We all had a bet going that someone would snatch Phyllis up quick after Charlie died. That's one fine woman. Never did figure out why she married Charlie. She always seemed like a bit of a wild card, and Charlie was the most uptight guy I've ever known. He was always one for rules and regulations. I don't know how you stayed his partner for so long. It would've driven me to drink."

I winced at that. I'd always thought the same thing, but it was upsetting to hear it coming from a total stranger.

"If I recall," Vince said, "everything drives you to drink. Charlie was a good cop, and he was a good partner. And I'm lucky I got a second chance with Phyllis."

"Oh, right," Jimmy said, his grin sly. "I forgot you two had a thing for a while after she and Charlie split up that time."

I squeaked and slapped a hand over my mouth. I never remembered my parents splitting up. But I do remember Vince always being a part of our lives. That nugget of information was definitely something to delve into later.

Vince shuffled his feet and changed the subject. "So who won the pot?"

"Stuart Marcel," Bruce growled. "Won three hundred lousy bucks. None of the rest of us figured you'd make a move again since you'd already ridden that merry-go-round."

"Some things are worth a second ride," Vince said. "Being a cop was some of the best years of my life, but it seems I wasn't able to leave all of it behind me. I've had some close calls recently. That's why I called you. There are very few people I can trust right now."

"You know you can trust us," Jimmy said. "Whatever you need, we're here."

"I appreciate that," Vince said, letting out a deep breath of relief.

"We heard through the grapevine that you started digging into the RICO case again," Bruce said.

"If you guys have heard it through the grapevine, I can only assume everyone has," Vince said. "That would explain the sudden close calls."

"There's no honor among thieves," Jimmy said,

shrugging. "The second you started sniffing around and re-questioning old informants, the information made its way down the food chain. Some of those informants are still active. So yeah, I'd say everyone knows what you've been doing at this point."

"That's why I need help," Vince said. "I'm being watched, and I can't move as freely as I'd like. Someone is trying to kill me."

"Man," Bruce said, his hands moving animatedly. "This case is twenty years old. And we closed it up tight. We sent people to prison. I don't think you want to open this can of worms. We knew back then we didn't round up all of the players. If you start digging you're going to have more than a close call. And I'm not ready to go to your funeral just yet."

"I wish I could let it go," Vince said, dropping his head slightly. "But we didn't get the right guy. And I have the proof. Or at least enough to start a new investigation. And apparently that's starting to piss some people off."

"Look, man," Jimmy said. "I love you like a brother, and we all worked our tails off on that case. It is what it is, and I'm telling you to leave it alone."

I held my breath. The tone had changed and the atmosphere in the room was heavy.

"Where'd you get proof?" Bruce asked.

"Charlie always had a feeling things were off with that case," Vince said. "I never believed him. I told him to drop it, just like you just did to me. But there was something that never settled right in

Charlie's gut about that case. Even after he retired he kept files and was still working the investigation on his own. I found all of his notes. And then I found the key."

"Key to what?" Jimmy asked, crossing his arms over his chest and leaning in slightly.

"A storage locker," Vince said. "And I hit pay dirt. I called you here because y'all worked the case with me and Charlie all those years ago, and I don't know who else to trust. I can't turn this over to the cops."

"Why not?" Bruce asked.

"Because Carmen de Salva had arms of his operation everywhere. Including the police department."

Bruce whistled. "You think the cops are dirty?" He and Jimmy shared a look.

"Somebody is," Vince said. "So will you help me?"

"Sure," Jimmy said, shrugging. "Where's this storage locker you found?"

"Whiskey Bayou," Vince told him.

"Then I guess we'd better go get it," Bruce said, squeezing Vince on the shoulder.

I saw the quick flash of steel and knew Bruce had blocked Vince from seeing Jimmy pull his weapon.

Jimmy pistol-whipped Vince in the back of the head, and I watched in horror as my stepdad dropped like a sack of potatoes.

"He won't stay out long," Jimmy said. "He always

did have a head like a rock. I've got zip ties in my trunk."

Jimmy and Bruce bent down and lifted Vince off the ground, and Jimmy threw him over his shoulder in a fireman's carry. I stayed low, but I needed to get as close as I could to the front of the house so I could at least get a license plate number.

I made my move as they were struggling to get Vince to the door, and I eyed the overgrown moss and grass a couple of feet from my stilt. I leapt without thinking, and my feet hit their target. It was short lived as the deceptive marsh gave way beneath my feet and I went down into the freezing water.

It turns out I didn't need Google after all. I figured out what a flotant was all on my own.

CHAPTER ONE

WEDNESDAY
Two Days Earlier...

On a scale of one to awesome, marriage was right up there with the Constitution, orgasms, and free samples at Costco.

I'd been married to Nick Dempsey for a little over a month, and we'd spent most of that time in a tiki hut on the water in Tahiti. Neither of us had tan lines, which should tell you a little something about how we spent most of our time.

On this particular morning, the marriage part of being married was amazing. It was the tiny person growing inside of me that I wanted to file a complaint to the manager about.

"Are you feeling better?" Nick asked, wrapping my hands around a mug of hot tea. "I brought you some toast."

"You're the best," I said and meant it. I tried not to look at the toast. I might as well have thrown it directly in the toilet.

"It seems like the least I could do, considering." The corner of his mouth twitched.

I'd hit the jackpot with Nick. He was movie-star handsome with dark hair and Irish blue eyes. He had a body sculpted by the gods, a wicked sense of humor, and he lived to serve and protect. And best of all, he'd chosen me.

"It seems unfair that men get to have all the fun of making the baby, but they don't get the pleasure of the vomiting, hemorrhoids, and irrational mood swings."

"Yeah," he said, his smile going wider. "It's a real bummer. I appreciate you taking one for the team."

"You're hilarious," I said.

"I've been told that before." He leaned down and kissed my forehead. "Are you going back to bed or are you getting up?"

I thought about it for a second. I was tempted to curl back up under the covers and sleep the morning away. Growing a person was exhausting. But I saw Nick was dressed in dark gray slacks, a royal-blue shirt, and a blue-and-gray-checked silk tie. He wore his shoulder holster and his badge was clipped at his belt.

We'd been home from our honeymoon for three days, and it had been magical. We hadn't told a soul we were back, and we'd spent our time watching movies, eating whatever we wanted, and making love. But today was his first day back at work, and the party had to end.

"I'm getting up," I said, tossing back the covers. "I'm told my energy will come back eventually."

"Yeah, in eighteen years," he said cheerfully. "Come on, you can walk me out."

He grabbed his sport coat, and I looked out the window at the miserable weather. We'd had nothing but clear skies and warm days in Tahiti, only to come back to the longest and coldest winter Georgia had ever had. It was still in the upper thirties, and the precipitation couldn't decide between drizzle and slush. Whatever was falling from the sky, the clouds were gray and it was cold and nasty.

I looked down at my flannel pajama pants and white T-shirt and stuck my feet into the slippers next to the bed. I shuffled after Nick down the stairs and watched him fill his to-go cup with coffee. He took a sip, grabbed his bag and his keys, and took his long wool coat from the hall closet.

I eyed him up and down, and then caught him staring at me. "Are you sure you have to go into work today?" I asked. "I could have all of those very nice clothes off of you in thirty seconds."

"As tempting as that is, you should probably brush your teeth first."

"Huh," I said, pressing my lips together.

"But I'll take a raincheck for later." He grabbed the umbrella out of the stand, and I opened the front door for him. "Oh, and I should probably mention that there's a taxi sitting out front. You might want to see what that's about."

I narrowed my eyes and looked past him into the dreary mist. Sure enough, there was a yellow taxicab idling behind his truck.

"How long has it been there?" I asked.

"It pulled up just as I was moving the truck from the garage."

"And you just left it there?" I asked, suspicious.

"I wanted to make sure you were up to visitors," he said. "And then I forgot it was out there."

"You've never forgotten a thing in your life, Nick Dempsey. You already know who it is, and you just don't want to deal with it."

He grinned and then leaned down to kiss my cheek. "I've got to get to work. Don't overdo it today." And with that, he flicked open the umbrella and hightailed it to his truck. He was at the end of the driveway by the time I got my feet in my rain boots and the slicker wrapped around me. I pulled the hood up and then stepped out in the wet, sloshing my way to the cab.

The taxi driver was a grizzled man in a news-boy's hat with an unlit cigar in his mouth. He was absorbed in a crossword puzzle and didn't notice me until I was almost at the window. I couldn't see into the back seat because of the tinted glass.

He rolled down his window. "I was wondering if we were going to have to wait here all morning," he said. "But your husband said you'd be out so I could be on my way. It's a long drive back to Port Canaveral."

"Port Canaveral?" I asked. "Who in the world would take a taxi to Savannah from Port Canaveral? That must have cost a fortune."

"She paid me a thousand bucks plus my fare," he said, chortling. "It'd be foolish to turn it down."

My blood ran cold. There was only one person who would pay a thousand dollars to spend hours in a cab in miserable weather. I peeked gingerly into the back window, expecting to see Aunt Scarlet looking like a wizened prune in one of the fur coats she enjoyed and talking the cabbie's ear off. Or at least trying to seduce him. Aunt Scarlet never let a younger man go to waste.

But she wasn't talking his ear off. Her head was slumped down on her chest and she was fast asleep. At least, I assumed she was asleep.

"Is she alive?" I asked, squinting to get a better look.

"Definitely," he said. "She's been snoring like a jackhammer."

Even as he spoke the words I heard a sound like a lawn mower starting, and her snores resonated through the cab and out the window.

"How have you listened to that for hours?" I asked. "I would've strangled myself by now."

"Eh," he said, shrugging. "I'm mostly deaf, and I just turn up the radio real loud. If you play Black Sabbath it sounds like she's part of the band."

"I'll remember that," I said. "I suppose I need to

take her off your hands." I was debating whether or not to pay him another thousand dollars to take her back to the boat dock. Having Scarlet in town was a double-edged sword. She was entertaining from time to time, but she almost always brought trouble with her.

I stared at her a few more seconds, continuing my internal debate, when her eyes popped open and her head snapped up. She let out a little scream at the sight of me staring at her through the window, and then she grabbed her chest.

The cabbie decided to be helpful and roll down her window. I shot him a scowl, but he rolled his own window up and went back to his crossword.

"What in the fresh hell is wrong with you?" Scarlet asked. "I could feel you staring at me. I got eyes in the back of my head. You don't survive the Nazis without having extra eyes. They used to watch me sleep all the time. I could lie still for hours. And then as soon as they'd drift off I'd jump up and snap their necks. I grew up wringing chicken necks. Human necks aren't much different."

"Hmm," I said. The cabbie had stopped his crossword and wasn't even pretending not to eavesdrop.

"My dad fought the Nazis," the cabbie said, over his shoulder. "Got his foot shot off."

"It happens," Scarlet said, shrugging. "I still got a bullet in my hip. It's been in there so long I figure it's holding things together. You sure you're married?"

"Forty-five years," he said. He grinned, showing a gap in his teeth.

"Hmmmph," Scarlet said. "Well, I'd guess you'd best hold on to her. You're not getting any younger."

I let out a sigh and opened the car door. "Let's get inside," I said. "It's wet and freezing."

"I was wondering if you had the good sense God gave you to get out of the rain," she said. "Pregnancy must be making you dumb. What are you wearing? Are you emo? I read all about them in *Teen People*. They have sex hanging upside down like bats."

I pressed my lips together and helped her out of the car. She was ninety pounds of woman and fifty pounds of fur coat. I didn't know how she was keeping herself upright. Her hair was flame red and covered in a plastic kerchief to protect it from the rain. She was carrying a Louis Vuitton travel bag and she shoved it at me while she said her goodbyes to the cabbie.

"Good luck," he said to me, and then drove off.

"Strange man," Scarlet said. "Not what he seems. I'd keep an eye on him if I were you. I memorized his license number just in case."

"Good thinking," I said, helping her up the three short stairs and to the front door I'd left open.

"Do you live in a museum? Why is this door so big? How come you don't have rocking chairs? What kind of house doesn't have a porch?"

I'd personally wondered the same thing. Nick's house wasn't the typical Savannah home. It was a big white elephant of a house—sleek and modern and square—with floor-to-ceiling windows at the front and the back so you could see all the way through.

I wasn't the sleek and modern type. I made Joanna Gaines look like a city slicker. And I loved a good wraparound porch with rocking chairs.

"Maybe I'll add one," I said. "Let's get you in and warmed up."

"I'm warm as a glass of brandy," she said.

I took off the slicker and rain boots and left them on the porch, and then I closed the front door behind us. "This is a nice surprise," I said. "Did you have your luggage sent to the hotel? What happened to your cruise?"

She moved into the main living area and stared at the giant black leather sectional and glass tables. There was art on the walls and rugs that were probably more expensive than the entire house. I hated the living room. The only redeeming thing about it was the view out the back. The main rooms of the house were sterile and cold, but Nick's office and the kitchen and most of the bedrooms were very cozy. It was like his interior decorator had split personalities.

I'd never actually told Nick that I hated this part of the house. I hadn't thought I'd ever be living here. At least not full time. But now that I was, it seemed like something I should mention.

"The ship caught on fire in South Africa," she finally said. "A little mishap in one of the staterooms. Lots of damage. They had to evacuate the whole ship. Took three days to get a new one and rebook the passengers for the rest of the trip."

"And why didn't you reboard?" I asked, suspicious.

"The captain recommended I sit this one out," she said. "He thought it'd be too strenuous for a woman my age to make that kind of trip alone, so they got me a ticket on a flight back to the US. I told him nonsense. I'm fit as a fiddle. It's age discrimination. I'm going to sue."

I pursed my lips. I could only assume she meant she'd burned down the ship and they'd told her not to come back.

"I like it better here anyway," she said, flicking her hand like it was no big deal.

Scarlet shrugged out of the fur, and I caught it just as it was about to hit the floor. And then she untied the plastic kerchief over her head. She'd taken to wearing wigs since the extensions hadn't worked out so great, and today's was a Sharon Osbourne wig in bright red.

She was dressed in one of her habitual jogging suits, this one terrycloth and the same color as her hair, with white racing stripes down the legs and jacket sleeves. She turned around and I saw the word *Juicy* written on her butt, and I couldn't do anything but shake my head.

"Your butt is a billboard," I told her.

She twisted her body so she could see her behind and smiled. "Men used to look at it all the time, but things aren't as high up as they used to be. I figured giving a little attention to the area couldn't hurt. I can still pop it like it's hot."

Nothing on Scarlet was as high up as it used to be, but more power to her. I hung her coat up in the closet while she got comfortable on the couch. She scooted all the way into the corner and her legs stuck straight out like a little kid's.

"I saw a couch like this once in a porno," she said. "It was an orgy couch. You have orgies here?"

"Not that I know of," I said, scrunching my nose in disgust.

"Just as well," she said, clicking her tongue. "I never enjoyed them much. I'm one of those women who likes to be the center of attention."

"No kidding," I said.

"I've decided I like being stateside," she said. "And it's important at my age to only do things you like. They don't even put ice in their sodas on the ship, and they changed their policy on topless sunbathing. I can't have tan lines. I bought a backless gown at Ralph Lauren to wear in the spring. If this blasted weather ever clears up."

"I'm going to put on a pot of tea," I said, so I didn't have to think about Scarlet's tan lines. "Do you want some?"

"No, but I'll take a mimosa," she said.

"We're fresh out of mimosas," I told her.

"I guess I'm still used to the cruise ship. I like my routine. What have you got that's the next best thing?

"I've got coffee and Bailey's or straight-up whiskey."

"I'll take the whiskey," she said. "It'll keep me warm when we go out later."

I felt a headache brewing right between my eyes. I hadn't planned on spending the day driving Scarlet to do errands. Especially not when I couldn't have a glass of wine at the end of the day.

"What are your plans today?" I asked. "Do you need a ride to your hotel?"

"I've got a couple of errands," she said. "But your guest room will be fine as far as accommodations. Do you have room service?"

"Guest room?" I asked, fear snaking down my spine. Nick was going to divorce me. Ours would be the shortest marriage on the planet.

"Are you daft, girl?" she asked. "Of course your guest room. I'm not going to bunk with you and Detective Hot Buns. I need my beauty rest, and newlyweds are far too active. I've been married five times, so I know about such things."

"Uh-huh," I said.

"I can't stay with your mother," she said. "I'd kill her, and I'm too old to go to prison. They don't let you kill people now like they used to. Social justice or some shit like that. My luggage will be delivered tomorrow."

"Umm, I..." I couldn't think of a thing to say. And I knew there was no use arguing. "I thought you always stayed at the Ballastone when you come to Savannah?"

"Well, there was a small hitch with that," she said. "Ever since I became notorious and wanted for the murder of Ugly Mo, I've been blacklisted at the Ballastone."

"That doesn't seem right," I said, pouring the whiskey over ice and then handing her the glass.

"Semantics," she said. "It could've been because the last time I brought Ugly Mo back to my room for a night of passion the walls and furniture incurred some damage. But I paid for it, so I don't see what the big deal is."

Ugly Mo had been a Savannah crime lord for as long as I could remember, and the police had never had enough evidence to charge him with anything. He tried to kill me, but I wouldn't have been able to prove it. A couple of months ago, someone took matters into their own hands and threw a Molotov cocktail through Mo's window and set him on fire.

No one had said the words out loud per se, but I was almost a hundred percent positive the person responsible was Scarlet. The justice system worked too slow to her way of thinking, and she wasn't one to let anyone hurt her family. It was probably best she moved around a lot.

"You know what I'd like?" she asked.

My tea finished steeping and I added milk and honey. "What's that?"

"I'd like some cake to go with my whiskey. That's just the thing on a morning like this."

Now that she mentioned it, I wouldn't turn down cake. "I'm going to shower, and I'll be back down in twenty," I said, carrying my tea with me to the stairs.

"Take your time," she said. "You look terrible. You must be having a girl."

"Why would you say that?" I asked.

"Because girls suck the beauty right out of you," she said.

"That's an old wives' tale."

She raised her brow and slurped her whiskey. "Not from where I'm standing."

CHAPTER TWO

"I'M LOOKING PRETTY HOT TODAY," SCARLET SAID, twirling in front of the full-length mirror in the mudroom. "We need a hot car to complement me." She looked me up and down and shook her head.

"I don't want to ride in that van of yours," she said. "That's a bad luck van. It's got Ugly Mo cooties. Ever since you had that van it keeps getting vandalized and you got kidnapped and held at gunpoint."

"Not to mention you wrecked my bathroom," I said.

"That too," she said, nodding. "But that was on account of how I had too many grits at breakfast. Grits keep you real regular."

"I'll remember that," I said. "I guess we can take the Audi today. I'm going to put the van up for sale anyway since I've retired from the PI life."

"Why would you go and do a stupid thing like that?" she asked.

"I'm pregnant," I said. "And I promised Nick I wouldn't do anything dangerous."

She *hmmph*ed and reapplied her bright red lipstick. "All I'm saying is that a little pregnancy wouldn't have stopped the women from my generation. Sometimes you get knocked up. That doesn't mean you don't sleep with the next Nazi to gain information. And it doesn't mean you can't stick your knife right in that soft spot at the hollow of the throat."

I led her out of the mudroom and under the attached portico that connected the garage. The Audi was parked in the first slot, and Scarlet was right. Sometimes you needed a sexy car to get cake.

The ride into Savannah was long and tedious between the traffic and the weather, and Scarlet slept most of the way, resting her head on the collar of her coat and snoring so loud I thought about putting her in the trunk.

The good news was the streets of historic Savannah weren't crowded with tourists. I dropped Aunt Scarlet off in front of Krazy Cakes and made sure she got in all right before I went to find parking.

"Thank you, Jesus," I said, finding a spot right on Reynolds Square across from the bakery.

East Congress Street looked like many of the other streets in downtown Savannah. The architecture was ornate and beautiful, and the attached buildings were being carefully restored one by one, with businesses and apartments put in to boost the economy. There were several newly renovated shops along the strip across from Reynolds Square, and the cake shop was one of them.

It sat on the corner, looking cute and tasteful from a distance. But the closer you got, the more the display windows came into view, and it was easy to understand why the shop was called Krazy Cakes. Suzanne had made both of the cakes for my wedding, and I'd been dreaming about them ever since. In her front window was a beautifully crafted historical home, complete with grounds and an iron fence in front of the property. And it was all made of cake.

Suzanne had a real talent. And then I looked a little closer. Inside the windows were different scenes, and I blinked a couple times to make sure my eyes weren't playing tricks. In one of the windows was a bloody mess of a man sprawled across a sofa, and in another window was a woman face down, a hatchet sticking out of the back of her head.

It was the Lizzie Borden house.

"Huh," I said, taking a step back from the window.

"Psst," I heard someone say.

My eyes were still glued to the delectable crime scene, and I was trying to figure out if I'd still eat it when I heard the voice again.

"Psst, Addison."

I looked up and around, trying to find the source of the voice and praying it wasn't the ghost of Lizzie Borden. She'd probably be pissed that I'd eat her murder cake. Most killers liked to show off their handiwork.

But it wasn't the ghost of Lizzie Borden.

"Rosemarie," I said, breaking into a smile. "What are you doing here? Why aren't you in class?"

"'Cause I quit," she said. "It's colder than an Eskimo pecker out here. Come inside where it's warm."

I looked through the cake shop window and saw Scarlet and Suzanne in deep discussion, and I caught Suzanne's eye and pointed to the shop next door.

It wasn't until I was actually walking into the shop that I realized what it was. *Valentine Weddings and Events.*

"No way," I said, my eyes going wide with surprise. "You did it."

"I sure did," she said. "I've been open a full week now."

Rosemarie's new business was gorgeous. Savannah was steeped in tradition, and you could throw a penny in any direction and hit someone who was considered "old money." They were picky about the places they did business, but if they liked you, it was like hitting a gold mine.

The floors were original and had been sanded and stained, and there were expensive rugs scattered about. The room was divided into two sections. On the left side was a conference table with large binders opened and different fabrics and place settings. The room could be closed off with pocket glass doors for privacy, but she had them pushed most of the way open.

There walls were old brick, and the rafters were exposed, and on the right side of the room was an old fireplace with a decorative plaster mantel. There was a sitting area in front of the roaring fire—two black velvet settees facing each other and black velvet armchairs with silver pillows.

I wasn't one to pry into people's personal finances, but Rosemarie had taught choir at James Madison High School in Whiskey Bayou. Teachers in Whiskey Bayou got paid slightly more than minimum wage and slightly less than the whores down on River Oaks Road.

"I can't believe you got the shop next to Krazy Cakes," I said. "That's prime historic Savannah real estate. It must've cost a fortune to get everything set up so quickly."

"It did, but I had some money saved up from when my great aunt Pearl died a few years ago. She owned a trailer park in Augusta and struck oil when they were digging the community pool. Made a fortune. I was the only one in the family she ever liked, so she left me a nice chunk of change and donated the rest to Apocalypse Now."

"The movie?" I asked, confused.

"No, it's a doomsday prepper group. They mostly live in underground bunkers, eat food out of packages, and use their poop to fertilize their gardens. It takes a lot of money for self-sustained living."

"Huh," I said, reaching for an apple fritter.

"And I got a real good deal on this space," Rosemarie said. "Suzanne owns four of the shops on this block, so she called the second the renovations were done and offered it to me. I'm leasing from her. This is wedding row. We've got cakes, a wedding planner, a florist, and a photography studio. And then the hair salon is down on the corner."

I was very familiar with the hair salon on the corner. Chermaine had chopped off my long locks into a cute pixie cut, and she'd put about thirty-two pounds of extensions in Aunt Scarlet's hair. Chermaine was a hair wizard.

"This is perfect," I said. "And you're going to do great. It's like one-stop shopping."

"That's the idea," she said. "I've already got a few weddings booked. I'm going to kick wedding ass, and then I'm going to take all my money and roll around on it naked and send pictures to my ex-husband. It's the least he deserves."

I'd known Roger Valentine only by reputation. He was a lot older than me in school, but he was a bully, an abuser, and philanderer. And everyone knew it. I'd always wondered why someone as sweet as Rosemarie had married him, but she'd never told me, and I'd never asked. But the ink on their marriage license had barely dried before they'd divorced, and Rosemarie had been single ever since. He'd clearly left an impression on her.

"My mother said last she'd heard he'd moved to Atlanta and had contracted syphilis," I said.

"I heard that too," Rosemarie said, nodding. "I wish I felt bad about that, but truth is I hope it rots his genitals off and buzzards scavenge his corpse."

"Wow," I said. "That's some imagery."

"I was an English minor," she said.

It was important to have goals, and I hoped Rosemarie achieved hers—both in her wedding planning venture and the demise of Roger.

"I didn't realize you'd come back from your honeymoon," she said.

I took off my rain boots and left them in the rack by the door, and I hung my jacket on the coat hook.

"We just got back," I said, not letting her know how long we'd been back so her feelings didn't get hurt. "Scarlet wanted cake for breakfast, so we thought we'd take a ride into town."

"Why is Scarlet in town? What happened to her cruise to Australia? I was supposed to visit her in November. I got my tickets and everything."

"You might check on a refund," I said. "I'm pretty sure Scarlet burned her ship down and now she's banned for life."

Rosemarie pouted and then blew out a breath. "Well, I suppose these things happen."

"Really?" I asked. "'Cause I can't imagine they happen very often."

I heard a *thunk* and Rosemarie screamed and put her hand to her chest. I turned and saw Scarlet on the other side of the door, her fur coat covering almost her entire body, and two big cake boxes stacked in her hands.

"It's just Aunt Scarlet," I said, going over to help her inside.

"Oh, thank goodness," Rosemarie said. "I thought it was a sasquatch."

"You got two cakes?" I asked Scarlet, taking the boxes from her. The scent of warm sugar wafted from the boxes and my mouth started watering. I was reminded I hadn't put anything in my stomach other than tea, and I was feeling much better now that the nausea had completely subsided.

"One is a cake," Scarlet said. "The other is pastries. Suzanne said you looked like you needed them."

"It's true," Rosemarie said. "You are looking a little peaky. And you've got dark circles under your eyes."

"Thanks," I said, taking the box of pastries over to the settee. "I'm so glad I used ridiculously expensive concealer to not cover them up."

"You must be having a girl," Rosemarie said. "They get jealous and zap all the beauty right out of you."

"So I've been told," I said, selecting a bourbon sugar ball from the box and popping it in my mouth.

I was feeling pretty raw regarding her comment on the dark circles under my eyes. Had I woken up at my best? No. But I'd done my best to ignore the morning sickness and put on a bright and cheerful face on a gloomy day.

With Nick back to work and me feeling sorry for myself, I'd known an attitude adjustment was in order. I just didn't understand why I was so sad. The weather made me sad, Nick getting to go to work made me sad, my dark circles made me sad, and the fact that there was a hole in my favorite underwear made me sad.

So I'd tried to brighten my day by wearing my black leggings and topping them with a yellow-and-black plaid skirt with pleats. I'd put on a matching yellow turtleneck and a black fuzzy vest. I thought it had been cheerful, but Aunt Scarlet had told me I looked like a bumblebee. I was a bumblebee with bags under her eyes.

I popped another bourbon sugar ball into my mouth and sniffed a little, trying to keep the tears at bay. I didn't feel quite so sad with the rush of sugar flowing through my veins.

I looked up to see both Scarlet and Rosemarie staring at me.

"What?" I asked.

"We've been talking to you for ten minutes," Rosemarie said. "You haven't heard a word we've said."

"If it's about the circles under my eyes or how I look like a bumblebee, then I don't want to hear it. I don't need that kind of negativity in my life."

"You've been in the doldrums ever since you

kissed that hunk you married goodbye this morning," Scarlet said.

"How'd you see that?" I said. "I thought you were sleeping."

"I told you, I've got eyes in the back of my head."

"Wait, why did you kiss Nick goodbye?" Rosemarie asked, confused. "I thought he was retiring from police work so he could run for his grandfather's senate seat."

"He is," I said. "But his grandfather's seat doesn't come open for another two years. Nick said he'll stay with the police department until the baby comes, and then he'll spend the next year or so campaigning for the seat."

I hoped Rosemarie didn't ask me how I felt about potentially being a senator's wife. I honestly had no idea. I mean, being a cop's wife was no walk in the park. I'd learned staying busy was key so you didn't constantly think about the million ways your husband could die. Plus, I figured the dangers of the job were probably a lot lower and the life expectancy was a lot higher for senators.

As far as the whole senator thing went, I was being supportive, but I couldn't really see myself in the role of senator's wife. I was presentable enough if the occasion called for it, and I knew which fork to eat with, but I was one of those people who could stick my foot in my mouth at any given moment. And if something embarrassing was going to happen to someone, chances are it was going to happen to me. Murphy's Law and I were well acquainted.

Scarlet pulled a fork out of her fur coat, and sat down on the settee opposite me. She opened the cake box and dug in.

"What's the matter with you?" Scarlet asked, licking icing off her lips. "And don't give me any crap about the baby. Women shoot out babies every day. Is it the hormones? I've heard they can make you crazy. I knew a woman who found out she was pregnant and ended up feeding her husband rat poison and then shaving her own head."

"That sounds like a bigger problem than hormones to me," I said. "Nick isn't in danger. I just feel out of sorts. Like I'm in someone else's body."

"I think your boobs are from someone else's body," Scarlet said. "They're huge."

"I kind of like that part," I said, looking down my shirt. "It's hard to explain. I've married the man of my dreams. We live in a nice house, and we have anything we could want, plus a baby on the way. But I'm...bored. Maybe that's not the right word."

"I don't think you're supposed to say you're bored until at least a year of marriage," Rosemarie said. "At least that's how it worked for me. But I'm probably not the gold standard when it comes to such things."

"I don't know," Scarlet said. "I've been married a bunch of times, and I got bored of a couple of them real quick. But I was never very good at picking husbands. I had a penchant for bad boys. And sometimes bad boys aren't the good kind of bad. Sometimes they're just bad."

"Isn't that the truth," Rosemarie said. "I learned the hard way that marriage isn't for everyone. And it's especially not for people who can't keep their peckers out of the whores down on River Oaks Road. Roger gave them so much money he had to send out 1099s at the end of the year."

"Any person who sticks anything into a whore on River Oaks Road needs a shot of penicillin and an exorcism," Scarlet said. "But you're right about one thing, they don't make bad money."

Rosemarie sighed. "I wish you had been my mother," she said to Scarlet. "I needed that kind of wisdom in my youth."

Rosemarie was working like a maniac while we were talking, comparing swatches of lace and pairing them with place settings and centerpieces.

She finished what she was doing and then came over to look inside my pastry box. I might have growled at her, but I decided to be polite. "Do you want that cinnamon twist?" I asked.

"I don't think so," she said. "I saw you lick the sugar off the outside five minutes ago."

Oh, yeah. I'd forgotten. "I'm eating for two," I said, picking up the cinnamon twist to finish it off.

"You're eating for thirty-two. That was a big box of pastries."

"I've got low blood sugar, and I've been a little down lately," I said. "Besides, it's Suzanne's fault. She gave me all the leftovers from the front case.

She would've thrown them out anyway. That's just wasteful."

"That's true," Rosemarie said. "Waste not, want not is what I always say. Sometimes I'll go in just before closing and see if she's got any sample cakes she didn't use for tastings. Then I'll go home, sit naked on my couch, watch the *Bachelor*, and eat cake. If that doesn't make you feel American, I don't know what does."

"God bless America," I said.

CHAPTER THREE

THE FRONT DOOR OPENED AND THE COLD AND drizzle rushed in. A whirlwind of color moved into the room, and a coat of crimson swung around legs almost as long as my whole body. Her lips and nails were painted the same scarlet as the coat. Suzanne could stop a crowd no matter where she went.

"Good morning, divas," Suzanne said dramatically, doing a catwalk turn around the room before unbuttoning her coat and letting it shrug off her shoulders and onto an empty chair. She was dressed in a tight leather skirt and a sheer black long-sleeved top that was covered by a leather corset vest. Her size twelve stilettos were studded and sported red soles. It wasn't the outfit I would've chosen to wear in almost freezing temperatures, but Suzanne could get away with anything.

"I've got that same outfit," Scarlet said. She'd finished her cake and was lying full out on the settee, still covered up in her fur coat. "I just don't wear it much because I like to breathe."

"Beauty takes sacrifice," Suzanne said. She took a seat in one of the chairs next to the fireplace and crossed her legs gracefully.

"How do you cross your legs like that without smashing your ding-dong?" Scarlet asked.

I dropped my head into my hand. "Kill me now," I whispered softly.

"Lots of practice," Suzanne said, her dark eyes full of laughter.

"Sometimes I wish I had a ding-dong," Scarlet said. "You can do lots of stuff with them."

"I've always thought so too," Rosemarie said. "A penis is a real game changer. You can pee in the snow. Get an erection. Get a good paying job. The possibilities are endless."

"When I was buying my cake this morning," Scarlet said. "I was admiring Suzanne's leather skirt. That sucker is tight, but she's got no bulges. She just shoves her balls into her body and tapes her penis to her butt. Isn't that amazing? And she doesn't even have a camel-toe. It's very impressive."

"Thank you," Suzanne said. "It took years to perfect my technique. I don't do it all the time, but sometimes you have to jazz things up to combat the gloomy weather." She looked at me and then over at the empty box of pastries sitting on the coffee table. "Girl," she said.

"I'm eating for two," I said, narrowing my eyes.

"I hear ya," she said. "Suzanne judges no one."

"Did you close the shop for the day?" Rosemarie asked.

"Sure did," Suzanne said. "Who would've thought we'd be this far into March and still having this awful weather? This is end-times weather. That's what I'm thinking. I try to make sure I stay in a crowd so I don't miss the Rapture. Sometimes when I'm in the shop and I don't have customers for hours on end I start to think I got left behind."

"Is that why you came to visit?" Rosemarie asked, her Kewpie doll eyes going wide. "What if we all got left behind?"

"I just don't wanna be by myself," Suzanne said. "My therapist said I've got to work on my co-dependency habits. I don't mind if I get left as long as I've got someone to talk to. I'm an extrovert."

"I figure that's why I'm still hanging around," Scarlet said. "I'd like to get zapped up. I watched a show where people got zapped up by aliens and that seemed pretty cool. They got probed and stuff, but I don't want to do any of that alien butt stuff." Then she looked at Suzanne. "No offense."

"None taken," she said. "I don't want to do any of that butt stuff either. I just like women's clothes, and I've found being a woman helps a lot within the cake business."

"That's real smart," Scarlet said. "I've always appreciated people who have good business acumen. That'll come in real handy if we get zapped up and need to find a way to make a living."

"I don't even know what's going on right now," I said to no one.

"I'm sure it's not the end-times," Rosemarie said, crossing herself. I shook my head. Rosemarie's been Methodist her whole life, but sometimes you needed a little extra oomph in your spiritual life. "God wouldn't end things just as I'm getting my business up and running."

"I don't know," Suzanne said. "I think God's punishing us."

"For what?" Rosemarie, Scarlet, and I asked together.

"Don't y'all watch TV?" she asked, shocked. "They got a documentary on just about everything nowadays. I like to consider myself educated on current events. We got pedophiles and politicians and serial killers and cults and God knows what other evil in the world. I figure we're about due for fire and brimstone or floods. I bought myself one of those floating survival pods just in case. It says it's rain and heat resistant, so I covered all my bases."

"Do they sell them on Amazon?" Rosemarie asked. "I like to get two-day shipping."

"I got mine at Costco," Suzanne said. "They got everything there. From birth to death to the apocalypse. They should advertise that for their memberships."

"Maybe I'll get one too, and we can be neighbors," Rosemarie said. "I'd need to get a doublewide on account of Baby and Johnny Castle."

"I'm gonna take my chances with the fire and brimstone," Scarlet said.

Suzanne looked at me and narrowed her eyes. "What's wrong with you today? Besides the fact that you just ate ten pounds of pastries. You look like a sad bumblebee."

"She's bored," Rosemarie said.

"Bored?" Suzanne asked. "Didn't you just marry the man of your dreams and spend the month in Tahiti?"

"The baby has made her loco," Scarlet said.

Suzanne pursed her lips and nodded. "This is why I'm glad I don't have the right equipment to have babies. I deal with pregnant ladies coming in the shop all the time wanting cake. Those hormones make you crazy as shit. I once had a lady go after my display case with a baseball bat. She ate almost everything in there before the cops came, glass and all."

"Bored is the wrong word," I said, sitting up straight. "And I'm not crazy. I don't know what's going on with me. But it doesn't help that I've been throwing up so much every morning I think I'm missing internal organs. I'm exhausted and fall asleep at the drop of a hat. My boobs are a size bigger and my bras don't fit. My husband is about to run for political office, and I'm not exactly Nancy Reagan. Plus, I'm out of a job and preparing to spend the rest of my life as Suzy Homemaker. And yesterday I cried because I ordered bacon at breakfast and when it came to the table it wasn't the right shade of brown."

"Ohhh," Suzanne said. "Well, that makes perfect sense."

"It does?" Rosemarie asked.

"I like the crazy theory," Scarlet said, belching lightly.

"Well, of course it makes sense," Suzanne said. "You're feeling like you don't have a purpose anymore."

I looked at her like she'd lost her mind. "Did you not hear anything I just said? I'm pregnant. I'm told it'll pass."

"Ridiculous," she said, flicking a crimson nail. "What you need is some excitement. A new challenge."

"What kind of a challenge?" I asked.

"You could redecorate the house, or go shoe shopping," Suzanne said. "The possibilities are endless."

"I wouldn't mind redecorating," I said. "Nick's house could use a woman's touch."

Scarlet snorted. "That's an understatement."

"Your choice of words is very interesting," Rosemarie said. "You just called it Nick's house. Which means you don't feel like it's yours."

I shrugged. "I guess you're right," I said. "It does feel like his house. When we were living together it wasn't such a big deal because it *was* his house. But now that we're married, it's supposed to be *our* house, but it still just feels like *his* house. Does that make sense?"

"Of course," Rosemarie said. "You just need to put your stamp on the place. That's all. Knock down a few walls, paint a few rooms. Buy out Pottery Barn. You'll feel better in no time."

"I used to work in construction before I made cakes," Suzanne said. "I'll be glad to help with whatever you need."

"Huh," Scarlet said. "I can't picture you on a construction site."

"Back then I wore boots and people called me Barry," she said. "I have a lot more fun now, and I get to eat as much cake as I want."

"That's what I want to do," I said. "I want to have fun and eat cake. What kind of career will allow me to do that?"

"Didn't you just have that career?" Suzanne asked. "If you liked being a PI then I don't understand why you don't just go and do that. You don't need an agency. You could put out your own shingle. I might have a storefront you could lease in a couple of months."

"As tempting as that is," I said, "I told Nick I'd put that life behind me now that we've got a baby coming." I felt my lip quiver. I *did* miss the thought of never being a private investigator again. I was good at my job. And after the wedding, everything had happened so fast I hadn't really had time to let it sink in that the career I'd poured my heart and soul into the past couple of years was gone.

"Are you crying?" Suzanne asked.

"No," I said, using my fuzzy vest to dry my tears.

"You'll feel better after we hit up Pottery Barn," Rosemarie said. "I always feel better when I spend money."

An awful sound was coming from the couch, and Rosemarie put one of the silver pillows over Scarlet's face to mute the snoring.

"That's unnatural," Suzanne said. "She's a danger to society."

"If you only knew," I said.

"Well, do something," Suzanne said. "This is the classy part of town. People are going to think they're living by the railroad tracks."

"She never sleeps long," I said. "She ate a whole cake."

"And two teacups of whiskey," Rosemarie said. "I saw her take the flask out of her coat. No telling what she's got in there."

My cell phone rang and I knew it was my mother since I used the beginning of "Bohemian Rhapsody" as her ringtone. I debated on whether or not to answer it.

"It's your mom," Rosemarie said excitedly, recognizing the ringtone. "Put her on speaker so I can say hello. I haven't seen her since the wedding."

Come to think of it, I hadn't heard from her since the wedding either. I figured she'd have texted at least a dozen times while we were on our honeymoon, but I hadn't even gotten one phone call.

"Hi, Mom," I said, answering. "You're on speaker."

"Good Lord," my mother said. "Is that a wood chipper?"

"Close," I said. "It's Scarlet."

Scarlet snorted at the mention of her name. "Wha—" she said, waving her arms. "Who's there? Why's it so dark in here?" Then the pillow toppled to the floor and she hissed like a vampire as the light hit her eyes.

"You're kidding," my mother said. "I thought she was on a cruise ship to Australia?"

"She burned it down," I said.

"Just my luck," my mother said.

Scarlet sat up and her Sharon Osbourne wig sat askew on her head. "Is that Phyllis?" Scarlet asked, narrowing her eyes. "Tell her we're busy."

"Ssh," I said, hushing Scarlet. My mother and Scarlet had never gotten along, but I wasn't sure when or why the rivalry had started.

"Phyllis," Rosemarie said, breaking in before Scarlet could say anything else. "I drove by your house the other day, and I love the twinkle lights in the gazebo and the new pond. You should get some ducks."

"I thought about it," my mother said. "You can have up to six poultry in the city limits. They'd be real cute waddling around the yard."

"And into the road," I said, imagining a mama and baby ducks being run over by my mom's neighbor's Cadillac. "Edna would mow them down without remorse. I saw her hit a crow out of a tree once with a pellet gun like she was Annie Oakley."

"She's always been like that," my mom said. "She's an unpleasant woman. I think she killed her husband."

I raised my brows at that nugget of information, but Mom didn't expound. "What's going on?" I asked.

"I need your help," she said.

There was something in the tone of her voice that had me worried. She was upset, and I hadn't noticed before. But the slight quiver in her voice was there.

"Sure," I said. "Is everything all right?"

"I think Vince ran away with another woman, and I need you to find him and bring him home so I can kill him."

CHAPTER FOUR

"OMG," Suzanne said. "This is just like *Real Housewives*."

Rosemarie, Suzanne, and Scarlet were all sitting on the edge of their seats, waiting to hear the sordid details.

"Who's that?" my mother asked.

"My friend Suzanne," I said. "She made the cakes at my wedding."

"I could use a good cake about now," my mother said. "But I'm all out of wine."

"How do you know Vince left with another woman?" I asked, trying to keep her on topic.

"Because he's been acting real sneaky ever since before your wedding. Spending lots of time on his computer in the study, and then he'd close his laptop if I came in."

"Maybe he's just got a porn addiction," Rosemarie said. "Some people are real private about that stuff."

"I wish it was as simple as that," she said. "But then I started finding receipts in his pants pockets, and one was for a hotel down in Miami. We don't know anyone in Miami. And then the other day I found a napkin in his pocket with the name Angelica on it and a phone number. I was going to confront him about it, but he made up this ridiculous song and dance about going fishing with his buddies at some cabin." My mother burst into tears.

"And then he kissed me goodbye and acted like nothing was wrong at all. The no-good, lying, cheating son of a whore. Vince has never fished a day in his life. I want you to find out who this Angelica woman is. She's probably young and beautiful. One of those Miami table dancers that looks like JLo, and knows how to twerk. I guess it's no fun being married to a woman too close to your own age. Who wants to deal with menopause and age spots?"

"I've always thought menopausal women were pretty great," Suzanne said. "'Cause then you don't have to deal with child support."

"True dat," Scarlet said, and they high-fived.

"Believe me," Suzanne said. "I've had a scare or two in my life."

I noticed Rosemarie's cheeks flame bright red. Suzanne and Rosemarie had gone to college together, and my investigative senses were tingling. There was definitely a story there.

"Look," I told my mother. "I'm on my way to your place now. I'll make a few calls, and get some information, and then we'll get to the bottom of this. Until there's absolute proof, you need to show him some trust. Vince has always been a good guy."

"All I want you to do is bring him back so I can know the truth," my mother said, sounding unusually calm. "And then I'm going to tie him up and show him why my sewing shears aren't to be used on anything besides fabric."

Rosemarie shook her head in sympathy. "I get that. Someone is always using them to cut paper."

"That's no reason to geld someone with them," I said.

"No," Suzanne said. "But I think the gelding is because of Angelica, though I wouldn't recommend it as a means to kill. Sounds awful messy."

"And also because murder is bad," I said, giving Suzanne a hard stare. "I'm on my way to your house right now. We'll get this all sorted out. Okay?"

"Thank you," my mother said. "I know you're retired now, but I didn't know who else to call. I figured it's best we keep this in the family for now. You know how the gossips are in this town."

I looked around at the circle of rapt faces and said, "Sure. It's all in the family."

I hung up and said, "I've got to go. Would you mind dropping Scarlet off at the house?" I asked Rosemarie.

"No way," Scarlet said. "I'm not missing this."

Rosemarie nodded. "What kind of friend would I be if I let you deal with this trauma all by yourself? This is your stepfather who's disappeared after all.

And your mama needs female support in a time like this. It takes a village. Besides, it's been a whole month since I helped you solve a case, and I'm going through withdrawals."

"Ohmigod!" Suzanne said, jumping to her feet. "I have the best idea ever. What if y'all went into business together. I can see it now." She waved her hand in an arc, as if she could see it on a sign. "Valentine and Holmes: Wedding and Investigative Services. Y'all would be the hit of Savannah. Because you know all the brides secretly want a background check on the guy they met off the internet. That's big business right there."

"That's brilliant," Rosemarie said. "Don't you think so, Addison?"

What I thought was I might be having a stroke. I didn't have any control over the muscles in my body so I couldn't shake my head or form words.

"She's speechless," Rosemarie said, doing a little shimmy in her stiletto boots.

"Ooh, I love a good dance party," Suzanne said. "Come on, Ms. Scarlet." Then they all started bumping and grinding and I was caught in the third level of hell. Scarlet's wig was still lopsided and her fur coat was slouched off one shoulder. It wasn't a good look for her. If there was going to be a Rapture, I couldn't think of a better time.

"I'd love to," I finally managed to get out. "But I promised Nick I wasn't going to take up PI work again."

"You're doing PI work for your mama," Suzanne reminded me.

"Yeah, but that doesn't really count," I said. "And Nick won't even know about it. I'm sure this is an open-and-shut case, and Vince will have a very good explanation. He's not the cheating type."

All three of them *hmmph*ed and shook their heads at my naïvety.

"Says the woman whose almost first husband was found in the back of a limo with a skank on your wedding day."

"That was a real good wedding," Scarlet said. "One of my favorites."

"I'm sorry I missed it," Suzanne said.

"The cake wasn't as good as yours," Scarlet said. "But the entertainment was top notch."

"Are you in the van?" Rosemarie asked me. "It'll be just like old times."

"No," I said. "I'm in the Audi."

Nick had bought me a sweet little Audi convertible that I rarely drove because I liked to think of myself as an independent woman who didn't want her man buying her expensive toys or making big decisions for her. But it was a sexy car, and I figured I'd better enjoy it while I could, because it wouldn't be too long until I was too fat to fit behind the wheel.

"Not a problem," Suzanne said. "I'm going to go make sure everything is closed up tight next door, and y'all meet me in the alley. We can take my van."

Rosemarie sighed. "I love your van. It always smells like cake."

That was good enough for me.

Ten minutes later I was seriously starting to wonder if my baby was making me crazy. My brain had obviously ceased to function.

I'd never seen Suzanne's cake van before. That was an oversight on my part, and I had no one to blame but myself. The van had been fully wrapped in bright images of her designs—wedding cakes, graduation cookies, and mouthwatering cupcakes. It would've been fine and dandy except the cupcakes had all been designed to look like body parts.

"She has a gift," Rosemarie said, taking the words right out of my mouth. "How do you think she does that? That's a good-looking penis."

"Don't say it," I said.

"Good enough to eat." And then she went into a fit of giggles.

Suzanne came out the back of her shop with her hands full and Rosemarie and I went over to help her. She had three cake boxes and an old Crate and Barrel paper bag.

"What is all this?" I asked.

"I figure the least we can do is give that woman a cake," Suzanne said. "Wives being cheated on deserve some cake. If I'd had time I would've made her one that looked like a gun."

"That's real thoughtful of you," Scarlet said.

"What's in the bag?" Rosemarie asked.

"She said she was out of wine, so I got the next

best thing. I got a couple of bottles of the amaretto I use to flavor the cakes. That ought to keep her busy awhile."

"You clearly don't know Phyllis," Scarlet said.

"I'll sit in the back," Rosemarie said. "I like to stretch out. And I want to take off my Spanx. They're squeezing my liver."

"I'm going to sit in the back too," Scarlet said. "I need to stretch out. Is there a bathroom in here?"

"No," we all said at once.

"Just checking," she said, and I hoisted her up into the back of the van with Rosemarie.

I sighed as I looked at my options for travel. Apparently that left me with the front seat. Now everyone in Whiskey Bayou could see I was driving around in a penis van.

"My mother is going to love this," I said.

The ride to Whiskey Bayou took more than an hour because of the weather. The drizzle was heavy, and the clouds were gray and angry. It wasn't supposed to get below freezing, but if it did the city would be shut down for days and the chances of finding Vince would be nil. The South didn't do well with any kind of winter weather, and for Mother Nature to have extended it into March was just downright cruel.

But the time we got to Whiskey Bayou, we were all ready to claw our way out and save our sanity. Scarlet had fallen asleep again, and her snores were shaking the van along with Black Sabbath. The cabbie had been right. Sometimes it did sound like she was part of the band.

"Oh, now," Suzanne said. "Isn't this the most darling town. Cute as a damned button."

"I tried to get you to come down here when we were in college, but you wouldn't do it," Rosemarie said.

"You weren't exactly selling it to me," Suzanne said. "And I don't remember you hurrying home every weekend. You usually bunked with me."

"You had better booze and a hot tub," Rosemarie said.

We heard a *thunk* and the snoring stopped, so we all peeked into the back to make sure Scarlet was okay. She'd slipped off her seat onto the floor and Rosemarie was helping her back up.

"I feel better," she said. "Nothing like a good afternoon nap. I always get sleepy after lunchtime."

"Or after your midmorning whiskey and cake," I whispered under my breath, but Suzanne heard me and chuckled.

"Bad Boys" started playing from somewhere in my bag, and I dug around, finding it on the very bottom while everyone else started singing along. I hesitated on whether to answer Nick's call with everyone in the van, but I figured there was some unwritten marriage rule about ignoring your spouse's calls. Especially when that spouse was a cop. The reality was in any given situation, it might be his last call.

"Hey," I said, plugging my ear with my finger so

I could hear better. "Are you in a tunnel? I can hardly hear you."

"Are people singing?" he asked.

"You don't want to know," I said. "What's up?"

"I caught a homicide," he said. "I'm on my way to the scene. Just wanted to let you know I don't know how late I'll be."

"Wow, that's a nice welcome back to work, huh?"

"You're telling me," he said. "You feeling better?"

"In a matter of speaking," I said. "I'm on my way to Mom's. She thinks Vince ran off with another woman, and she's freaking out a little."

"That doesn't sound like Vince," Nick said.

"I'm guessing Mom thought that too until she found Angelica's phone number in his pants pocket and hotel receipts."

"Yikes," Nick said. "Have fun with that. I'll see you when I see you."

"Ask him," Rosemarie hissed.

"What?" I asked, confused. "Ask what?"

"About redecorating the house," she said.

"Who are you with?" Nick asked. "It sounds like you're at a party."

"I guess you could call it that," I said. "By the way, it's a shame you didn't stick around this morning to say hi to Scarlet. She's going to stay with us for a while."

There was silence on the other end of the line. Then he said, "There's a lesson to be learned in there somewhere."

"You think?" I asked. "Scarlet wanted cake for

breakfast, so we drove into the city and stopped at Krazy Cakes. And it turns out Rosemarie's new wedding planning business is right next door."

"It sounds like you've had a busy morning," he said.

"You have no idea." I looked in the back seat and Rosemarie was still singing "Bad Boys" in her operatic soprano. "I was in the Audi, so when Mom's call came in Suzanne volunteered her van so we could all go console my mother. We're bringing her booze and cake."

"So let me get this straight," Nick said. "You, Scarlet, the cake lady, and Rosemarie are all in a cake van to go visit your mother?"

"That about sums it up."

"She's going to love that," he said.

Suzanne was motioning for me to ask him about decorating the house, and I finally found the courage.

"Can I ask a favor?"

"After the morning you've had, you can ask for anything," he said. "But do it quick because I'm almost at the crime scene."

My palms were sweaty and I rubbed them on my leggings. Nick was a man. Which meant he didn't like change, despite his assurance that I could ask for anything.

"I was wondering..."

"Yeah?"

"I was wondering if maybe it'd be okay to do

some redecorating in the house," I said in a rush. "You know, so it feels more like it's mine too."

Nick was silent for a few seconds. "Babe, the house is yours as much as it is mine. Do what you like. As long as I have a soft bed and the refrigerator doesn't move, I'm good with it. With the way my job is, it's not like I get to spend a lot of time there anyway. I've got to go. There are bodies in the yard, and the media is going nuts."

"Fun," I said. "Be safe." And I hung up.

"What'd he say?" Rosemarie asked.

"He said the house was mine to do as I wanted." Or at least that was close enough to what he said in my mind.

"I love a good house renovation," Suzanne said. "I watch the shit out of Chip and Joanna. I can shiplap like nobody's business."

Suzanne kept oohing and ahhing over the cuteness of the town, and I tried to look at Whiskey Bayou through her eyes. I guessed the *Welcome to Whiskey Bayou, The First Drink's on Us* sign and the cobblestoned roads were charming, and the railroad graveyard had a certain artistic sense to it that threw you back to a simpler time.

We didn't have much of a downtown—a few specialty boutiques that came and went with the times and the Good Luck Café, which hadn't gone anywhere in seventy-five years. Technically, the Walker Whiskey Distillery was in the dead center of town, which is what put Whiskey Bayou on the map, so to say, before prohibition. In a weird turn of events, Scarlet gave me the distillery as a wedding gift. I wasn't really sure what I was supposed to do with it, but I'd had a couple of people ask to rent it out for their weddings, so Nick was looking into insurance and all the other adult things that came with owning property.

In normal towns, there would've been a courthouse in the middle of the town square, but since the distillery occupied that spot the courthouse faced directly across from it. The Methodist church was on another side of the square and then the fire station and police department rounded it out on the last side of the square.

My mother lived a block past the fire station on an old residential street that dead-ended into the bayou. The houses were all on double lots, so you weren't too close to neighbors. My mom had grown up in the house, and the same families tended to stay in houses for generations and expand however they could. Whiskey Bayou was landlocked, and real estate wasn't easy to come by.

"Huh," Suzanne said as she pulled up to my mother's house. "Looks like one of those cottages in the fairytales where small children go to die. And it's even got the General Lee out front."

In a fit of rebellion, my mother had taken the insurance money my dad had left her and bought an exact replica of the General Lee. I wasn't sure why. I only knew that my dad would've hated it, which I'm guessing is why she'd done it. My parents had a complicated marriage.

"Yeah, sorry about that," I told her.

"Sugar, I'm a black cross-dresser from the South. I've seen everything."

My mother had the front door open before we got out of the van, and there was a shell-shocked look on her face. I guess we did draw attention, even past the van. Rosemarie and Scarlet crawled out of the back, and the look my mother gave me was full of accusation and betrayal. I shrugged in apology and held up the cake boxes, hoping she'd take the peace offering.

"Mom, this is Suzanne," I said. "I don't know if you got to meet her at the wedding. She made the cakes."

"I brought chocolate cake and amaretto," Suzanne said.

"We're here for moral support," Rosemarie said, giving my mother a hug before hurrying inside.

"I just came for the entertainment," Scarlet said. "I figure this serves you right after you killed Charlie."

I raised my brows at that bit of information and looked at my mother. She rolled her eyes and said, "I didn't kill Charlie. He died of a heart attack."

"*Hmmph*," Scarlet said. "So you say."

"So everyone says," my mother said.

Scarlet went inside with the others and I was left alone with my mother. I felt like I hadn't really gotten to know my mother until after my father died. Growing up, she'd been a stickler for rules and proper etiquette. Since his death, she'd been a wild card of personalities.

"Don't think I won't pay you back for this," she said. "I've been doing Tae Bo all morning to get rid of some of my anger. I can't promise I won't drop-kick Scarlet into next week."

"She's just an old lady," I said.

"She's the devil," my mother said.

"I heard that," Scarlet said from inside the house.

"See," my mother whispered, her eyes going wide. "Are those cupcake penises on the side of that van?" she asked, squinting toward the road.

I moved past my mother into the tiny house. Growing up had been a challenge with only two bedrooms and one bathroom. My father had decided he couldn't stand the constant fighting between me and my sister in our teenage years, so he had a third bedroom built on. When we moved out, he turned it into his office.

"We brought cake and booze," Rosemarie said, patting my mother on the back and leading her to the dining table. "We'll get all this sorted out. You've got nothing to worry about. And if you ever decide to get married again, I've got you taken care of. I'll give you a real good discount."

Suzanne made herself at home, getting out plates and silverware and the aperitif glasses like we were having a tea party. She put the kettle on for me, and then went about the business of cutting cake. I was technically still full from the pastries I'd eaten, but Suzanne had brought a hummingbird cake, along with the chocolate, as one of the selections, and only a fool would turn down hummingbird cake. It was my favorite.

Scarlet took off her fur and tossed it over the back of the couch, and then stared at the cake, sucking her cheeks in. "You got any vegetables? If I eat that cake, it's not going to be a pretty ride out of here. I need something to cleanse my palate." Scarlet didn't bother to wait for an answer, but went into the kitchen and started rummaging around in the refrigerator.

"Maybe you could start at the beginning," I told my mom after she'd tasted her first bite of cake.

"I told you," she said, shrugging. "Vince is stepping out on me with some two-bit ho from Miami. I don't know how he met her. We've never been to Miami. When I suspected him of cheating, I did a Google search and I found a list of signs that your man is cheating on you. He's been taking frequent trips to see his buddies," she said, holding a finger up. Then she put up a second finger. "He's real secretive about his phone, and he's always texting." Her third finger popped up. "He's spending money without telling me. I used to be an accountant. Does he think I don't check the bank balances and credit card statements? What kind of dummy does he think I am?"

She burst into tears and laid her head down on the table. I felt bad for her. I really did. My parents were devoted to each other, but I wasn't ever sure they had a happy marriage. What she had with Vince had felt like the real thing.

"You're not a dummy," I assured her. "If he's cheating on you then we're going to get the proof."

"Yeah," Rosemarie said. "And then we're going to get revenge. I set Roger's car on fire."

"I remember that," Scarlet said. "That was a real doozy. It takes real skill to make a fire that lasts with that kind of heat."

"Thank you," Rosemarie said, pinkening slightly. "I watched a video. The key is to get some magnesium and sprinkle it all in the car first. It makes the flames real pretty."

"Good Lord," Suzanne said, shaking her head. "I cannot be privy to this. You know who's gonna go to jail if we get caught planning a revenge car torching. And I can't go to prison. I've become accustomed to the creature comforts in life."

Rosemarie rolled her eyes. "You grew up with the creature comforts in life." Then Rosemarie looked at me and said, "Suzanne's parents live two doors down from Nick's parents."

"Oh," I said. And then I grinned and Suzanne laughed.

"I'm a rebel," she said. "I've got mommy and daddy issues, and my therapist says I'm acting out by dressing as a woman."

"I don't know why you're paying that therapist all that money," Rosemarie said. "That seems kind of obvious to me."

"I like the company," Suzanne said. "He's a good conversationalist."

"I don't mean to be rude," my mother said. "But maybe we could get back to my cheating husband issues."

"Right," I said. "How long do you think the affair has been going on?"

"I don't know anything right now," mom said. "We're still newlyweds. How can he be tired of me already?"

I shot Scarlet a look to keep her from commenting, and she gave me the signal of zipping her lips.

"He started off by just acting distant," mom said. "I figured he had something on his mind, but thought he'd talk about it eventually. I was married to a cop long enough to know when to let things simmer and when to poke and prod.

"But Vince isn't like Charlie. He's always been very open about his life and career. I mean, we've known each other thirty years, so he was really just filling in a lot of the blanks. I've not really touched your father's office since he died, but I did go in a few years ago and box up all his old papers and anything personal, and I shoved it in the closet.

"Vince decided to turn the room into his man cave, so he started cleaning things out and getting his electronics set up."

Porn, I saw Rosemarie mouth out of the corner of my eye, but I kept my attention on my mother.

"I mean, Vince and Charlie were as close as brothers for a lot of years," mom said. "So I figured he started seeing all of Charlie's stuff and it made him sad. Vince even slept in the office that night. He completely shut me out.

"I thought everything had gone back to normal when he took all of your father's things and put them out in the shed with his other stuff. Lord, Charlie was a packrat. He had boxes of old case files, body armor, bullets, guns...you name it. If they made something new for law enforcement, then he had to have it. It's all out there."

"You've got guns in the shed?" I asked, wide eyed.

"Don't worry," she said, waving a hand. "I've got plenty in here too. You can never be too careful with all the lunatics and perverts running around. I ran one of those sex offender searches on the computer, and you can throw a rock and hit one."

"What if all the perverts storm the shed and plan an attack on the house?" I asked. "Is it at least locked?"

"Of course it is," she said. "That was your dad's man cave before man caves were a thing. He never let anyone in there who wasn't a cop. Even after he died I never touched the place because I was afraid he'd come back and haunt me. I was thinking about just burning the whole thing to the ground and letting insurance pay to build me a she shed. I'd like a private place to do my morning yoga and drink my afternoon wine."

"I've got a she shed," Suzanne said, pressing her

lips together primly and cutting more cake slices. "Except mine has a pool table and a flat-screen TV."

"And a pinball machine," Rosemarie said. "You always did have all the good toys."

"Don't you know it, sugar," Suzanne said, winking at Rosemarie.

Seriously, I was going to have to delve into their history a little more once my mother wasn't having a crisis. Because there was some definite chemistry between the two.

My mother sipped at her amaretto and stared out the window forlornly. Scarlet had found a bag of celery and was dipping it in a jar of peanut butter, and she passed them over to me. I hated to say it, but I needed a break from cake.

"What happened next?" I asked my mom.

"We just started drifting apart," she said. "It's like he decided to start living his own life and leave me out of it. Then he started taking these little trips. Weekend camping trips with the boys. A drive to Biloxi to hit the casinos. A trip to watch a basketball game. Stuff like that. And then he told me one of the cops who was friends with him and your dad was really sick and in the hospital, so he took off for four days to go visit him."

"Ugh," Rosemarie said, shaking her head. "I heard the same kind of lies from Roger. I knew from the start he was lying and cheating on me. It's in a wife's DNA to know. The second he dipped that wick it was like a switch had been flipped."

"Roger was a horse's ass," Suzanne said. "I told you not to marry him."

"Everyone told me not to marry him," Rosemarie said. "But I was looking for an escape and I found it."

"It's when they stop having sex with you that you really know something is up," Suzanne said.

My mother nodded in agreement. "Nothing but excuse after excuse," she said. "*Not tonight, Phyllis, I'm too tired.*" She rolled her eyes. "Or my favorite, *Put your clothes back on, we're in public.*" I tried to keep my expression blank, but I wasn't sure I was succeeding. "That's when I knew something was wrong. That man has never told me to put my clothes back on in his life. I don't do yoga for nothing, you know."

"Age only improves your skills," Rosemarie said wisely. "These middle-aged men don't know what they're missing with those toothpick twenty-year-olds. I love dating older men. Older men know all kinds of things."

"Meh," Scarlet said. "They're good for sex, but if you get them too old then they just want to boss you around. My first husband was thirty years older than me. He taught me the ways of the world and where my G-spot was. I always say that every husband has a purpose. Of course, I'm only into shacking up now. There's not too many men older than me, and all the rules have changed. I don't want anyone to marry me for my money. Look at what happened to Elizabeth Taylor."

"I bet you went crazy once he started holding out," Suzanne said. "There's nothing like a woman scorned. They can dig up information on anybody."

My mother nodded. "You pick up things after being a cop's wife for more than twenty years. I went through his social media accounts and his phone records, but he's not really a social media guy. He thinks it's a gateway to criminal behavior."

"He's not wrong," Rosemarie said, and then belched lightly. "I think I might throw up." She looked a little pale, and there was a sheen of sweat on her upper lip.

"She's got the cake sweats," Scarlet said. "You've got to know your limits. You're a grown woman."

"I just need some water," Rosemarie said.

My mother got up and brought her back a bottle of water, and everyone moved their chairs back a few inches so as not to be in the line of fire or get in her way if she needed to run to the bathroom.

"Did you find anything in his phone records?" I asked.

"Nothing I knew what to do with," she said. "I've got numbers, but I don't know who they belong to or what he was texting about. I wrote them down," she said, passing me a list on a torn piece of notebook paper. "I also checked out the credit card statements and found the hotel in Miami, and then I found Angelica's phone number on a napkin in his pocket."

"Where was the napkin from?" I asked.

"The Four Seasons," she said. "He's certainly

never taken me to the Four Seasons, but I guess he can only splurge the fancy stuff for his whore."

"Why don't you give me everything you've found," I said. "Can you log online and print off his log of phone calls and texts? I can do a reverse search and see if I can find out who they belong to. Are you going to be okay here by yourself?"

"Oh, sure," she said. "I'm armed and sometimes I like being by myself. I can sit around in my underwear and drink wine whenever I want to. Retired life is the best. Everyone should do it. But sometimes I like to have intelligent conversations and sex. That's the whole point of marriage—having someone readily available for both at a moment's notice."

"I'll remember that," I said.

CHAPTER FIVE

Rosemarie and Suzanne had a little too much amaretto, so I ended up driving the penis cupcake van back to Savannah. Rosemarie and Suzanne had fallen asleep in the back seat almost as soon as we'd left my mother's. Scarlet sat in the front with me, and she gossiped about the families who'd lived at almost every house we passed.

"That was Evelyn Pickering's house," Scarlet said, pointing to the old white Victorian hidden from the road by a bunch of trees. "Men used to shimmy right up that drain spout to her bedroom while her husband was away at war. We called her Skeevy Evie. And when Milton came back after he'd been wounded at Normandy, I guess she forgot to send out a memo to her men, because one night Clyde Barker climbed up and Milton shot him right in the face."

"Amazing," I said, slowing the car down as we passed the house. I'd heard the story a million times since I was a kid, but I'd always been fascinated by the house. There was a presence there, and everyone could feel it.

"Didn't even go to jail," Scarlet added. "I tell you, those were the good old days. Somebody done you wrong, you just pop a cap in their ass and bring a company salad to the wake. Sometimes you make a move on the widow. There weren't as many fish in the sea back then either."

I'd always been fascinated by Scarlet's stories of the war years. As kids Phoebe and I had sat at her feet, shelling peas and listening to her, and I'd always felt like I'd been born in the wrong generation. I loved the music, the clothes, and the fierce determination to live the American dream.

"Let's get a move on," Scarlet said. "I'm late for my nap."

"You've had two naps since we left the house this morning," I said.

"Yeah, but this is my afternoon nap," she said. "My afternoon nap is the good one because I get to have a sidecar beforehand."

The rain had steadily picked up, so I wasn't too self-conscious about driving around in the van. It's not like anyone was standing outside to witness.

I dropped Suzanne and Rosemarie back at the cake shop, and then I ran to get the Audi from where I'd parked so I could swing around and pick up Scarlet.

It wasn't yet three o'clock, and I figured Nick would be tied up with his homicide for a good while longer. That gave Scarlet plenty of time for her nap and me plenty of time to run a cursory background check.

I'd only planned to drive by the detective agency on the way home, but it seemed like a sign when I saw the empty parking space right in front.

"Oh, good timing," Scarlet said. "I've got to go to the bathroom. That celery is running right through me. I need to unloose this caboose, if you know what I mean."

"I got it," I said and sighed. I got out of the car and went around to help Scarlet out, but she was already halfway out the door and onto the sidewalk.

"My friend Ernie gets to poop in one of those bags," she said. "Seems pretty convenient to me. Sometimes I wish I could poop in a bag, but I've got pipes of steel."

I wondered if I'd ever get to the age where I felt comfortable talking about my bowels. I was thinking that would be a negative.

I took Scarlet by the elbow and locked the door of the car. Rain dripped off the hood of my raincoat and I stared at the front of the building where I'd had some of the best memories of my life. I thought the detective agency would look different somehow. But it was the same.

Kate had discreetly put the agency up for sale right around the time of my wedding, but there weren't a lot of qualified buyers who could afford the building, the staff, and uphold the reputation that came with the McClean Detective Agency.

Kate hadn't wanted to make a big fuss, so it was mostly business as usual until it was sold, at least for the clients she had on retainer.

Even the building looked sad. The red brick seemed gray and drab in the rain, and the ivy that trailed up the side of the building sagged.

"Didn't you hear me, girl?" Scarlet said, jerking her elbow away from me. "I have to poop." And then she sprinted up the stairs and into the building.

She said it so loud I immediately looked around to make sure no one heard. There was a man who'd been running to his car from the adjacent building, but he'd stopped in his tracks to stare. I smile and waved, and then followed after Scarlet. I was so mortified I didn't even see Kate standing under the stoop.

"You going to stand out there all day looking sorry for yourself?" Kate asked.

"I was thinking about it," I said.

"Well, do it in here," she said. "It's warmer and more comfortable."

"Tell me that again after Scarlet finishes wrecking your bathroom."

Kate winced. "Maybe I should just have the building bulldozed," she said.

"It's definitely an option," I said, and walked up the stairs and into the warmth.

It looked the same on the inside—the plush and expensive furniture in the lobby, the original hardwood floors, expensive paintings, and a large Ushaped desk that Lucy Kim helmed with an iron fist. It might have looked the same, but it didn't feel the same. It felt—empty.

Kate had built a good business over the past several years. People all over the world sought her out because she was the best. I had no idea why she'd hired me other than a lifetime of friendship.

"Where's Lucy?" I asked. "I thought she was your top contender for buying the agency?"

"She decided she didn't want to be an owner," Kate said, shrugging it off. She might have shrugged it off, but I could tell she was worried. "Lucy wears a lot of hats, and she was working here at first as a favor for Savage. And then she stayed because she was entertained by this line of work. I have a feeling her normal workday isn't always so enjoyable. She only ever worked for me part-time."

"Really?" I asked. "'Cause it seemed like she was always here. What's her other job?"

Kate just smiled. "If I told you I'd have to kill you."

"That never stops being hilarious," I said, rolling my eyes.

"Hey, if you want be privy to all the secrets, then you should buy the place."

My mouth dropped open as I watched Kate walk down the hall to her office. She knew how to dangle a carrot better than anyone I knew. Of course, she'd known me since grade school and had been putting up with my shenanigans for the same amount of time. And now all I could think about was owning the agency and devouring every word of Lucy Kim's employment file like it was a dime store romance novel.

"You'd sell it to me?" I asked, following behind her.

She laughed. "I have a feeling Nick might have something to say about the matter. I've seen your paychecks, so I know it's not you who'd be paying for it. I'm very expensive."

"I could make a joke there," I said, taking my raincoat off and hanging on the tree stand.

"I'm sure you could," she said. "Exactly how much money does Nick's family have?"

I shrugged. "I don't know. A lot, I guess. He's got a trust fund from both sides of the family, and he's got some property here and there. We've never really talked about it."

"You never looked at property records or anything like that?"

"That would be a misuse of company property," I said, primly.

Kate laughed, a full-out laugh that made me smile. "Nothing showed up under his name, huh?" she asked.

"It's all tied up in the trust," I said.

She wiped her eyes and then looked me up and down. "Why are you dressed like a bumblebee? And why aren't you home partaking of wedded bliss?"

"You ask a lot of questions for a woman who never answers any," I said.

It was my turn to look her over. I hadn't seen her since just after the wedding when we'd gone to see Savage in the hospital. I'd noticed the last year or so Kate had been under a tremendous amount of stress. It hadn't helped that she'd found out about her husband's gambling addiction, or that when she'd hired me, she'd unofficially gotten Rosemarie and Scarlet.

Kate had always been cute as a button. Her hair was blond and she'd had it cut recently so it was a little shorter than usual, but she still wore the same black headband to keep the hair out of her face. Kate was a lost cause in the fashion department. I'd been trying for years to spruce up her wardrobe and get her to wear lipstick.

She still wasn't wearing makeup, but the line that had seemed like a permanent addition in between her eyes had disappeared. She looked— rested. It was the first time I'd seen her like that in years.

"You look good," I said. "I mean, not that outfit though. Are you buying suits from the Hillary Clinton collection? I've never actually seen a pumpkin-colored suit in person before. Where's your body? You're young and hip. Maybe when you finally sell the agency we can have a party and burn all your ugly suits."

"I'm not taking fashion advice from an insect," she said.

"It's cute," I said, looking down at my attire. There was a blob of crème from the éclair right in the middle of my boobs. "I had pastries for break-fast and cake for lunch."

"That would explain why you look like you're jonesing for a hit," she said. "Are you going to tell me why you're sitting in my office instead of boinking your very fine husband?"

"Believe me," I said. "There has been no lack in that department. You should see how even my tan is."

"I'll pass," she said, taking a seat on the couch instead of behind her desk.

"Nick went back on duty today," I said. "He caught a homicide."

"There's no shortage of those around here," she said. She kicked off her shoes and lay back on the couch, and my mouth fell open.

"What are you doing?" I asked. "Are you sick? Are you having a stroke?"

She looked at me out of the corner of her eye. "I'm just lying down."

"Like, for a nap?"

"I've been taking one almost every day," she said, the corner of her mouth tilted in a smile. "Naps do wonders for the disposition. I wish I'd been taking them for years."

"Scarlet says the same thing," I said. "I've never seen you take a nap. At least, not since kindergarten, and even then you never closed your eyes. It was freaky. What's wrong with you?"

She laughed and I became even more worried.

"Nothing is wrong with me. I'm just taking the time to enjoy this very comfortable couch."

"It is comfortable," I agreed. "I've snuck in and taken a couple of naps on that thing. You should take it with you after you leave."

"Hmm," she said, sliding her hand across the leather. "Do you think Scarlet's okay?"

"I'm not sure I'm brave enough to check," I said. "But if she doesn't come back in a few minutes I'll go check on her."

"I've got a gas mask in my desk you can use."

"Really?" I asked. And then I narrowed my eyes at her. "Kate McClean, don't think because you're being all pleasant and making conversation that I don't know what you're up to. Don't change the subject. I want to know what's going on with you and why you're in such a good mood."

"Because this transition to sell has been the least amount of work I've done in years," she said. "I'm free. At least for the most part. It's like being on vacation. I'm not having to deal with any new clients or crazy people looking to catch their spouse having an affair. I'm not up to my eyeballs in paperwork every night or dealing with insurance companies or chasing down corporations who don't like to pay bills on time. This isn't exactly the kind of business people use unless something is going wrong in their life. It's kind of a bummer. This is the kind of job that if you do it too long you lose all faith in humanity and you stop trusting anyone. And I've definitely been doing it too long."

"Wow," I said. "I had no idea you were so miserable."

"Not miserable," she said. "Just challenged. It's taken a while to figure out my priorities. Mike and I want to travel. And the agency has been good to me over the years. I want to enjoy the fruits of my labor. I've had a couple of government agencies send out feelers to see if I'd be interested in consulting, so I'll use this time to think about my future. You understand now that you've got Nick in your life. There's nothing you wouldn't do for him, or for your marriage."

"That's true," I said. "Which is why I gave up PI work."

"No you didn't," Scarlet said, coming into the room. "Whew, do I feel better. Kate, you might need to knock a few bucks off that sale price for this thing. Maybe I should just write you a check. Do you take Venmo?"

"I'll just light a candle," Kate said. "It'll be fine."

"Don't count on it," Scarlet said. "We set a latrine on fire during the war and it took out half the battlefield."

Kate looked back at me. "What's this about you not giving up PI work? I don't show you as working on any active cases. What's going on?"

I sighed. I'd never been any good at keeping secrets from Kate, so I figured I might as well tell her. "I'll tell you, but you can't let my mother know you know."

Scarlet *hmmph*ed. When we turned to look at her she said, "Don't mind me."

"I won't say anything," Kate said.

"Mom thinks—"

"All I'm saying is that everyone already knows," Scarlet said. "If Vince has been skipping out on her for more than a month then everyone in Whiskey Bayou and their dog knows. Just interview Edna from next door. Nosy old bat. I bet she knows what's up."

It wasn't a bad idea, and I added it to my mental to-do list.

"Vince is cheating on your mom?" Kate asked, wide eyed. She scooted up on her elbows and propped pillows behind her head so she could see me.

"I wanted to tell it," I said, looking at Scarlet.

"You were taking too long," she said. "I could die by the time you get to the end of the story. Sometimes you've got to rip the Band-Aid off."

"You just wanted to spread the gossip," I told her.

"That too," Scarlet said. "Carry on. I won't say another word." She zipped her lips and mimicked throwing away the key.

"We don't know if he's cheating for sure," I said, and Scarlet *hmmph*ed again. I just ignored her this time and went on. "But the evidence against him is pretty damning. Mom's got phone records and credit card bills."

Kate winced. "That just doesn't sound like Vince. He's a good guy. Steady as they come."

"I would've thought so too," I said, shrugging.

"What'd he say when she confronted him?" Kate asked.

"She hasn't confronted him yet," I told her. "But she says it's been going on about a month. He met some woman named Angelica at the Four Seasons in Miami."

"Pricey," Kate said, raising her brows.

"I've got the woman's name and phone number. I was going to run a reverse search and do a little digging. Rosemarie just wants to set his car on fire."

Kate grinned. "I remember when she did that to Roger. That was a doozy of a fire. Burned for days. Made the papers all the way in Savannah."

"All my program subscriptions have expired now that I'm not with the agency," I said. "Can I borrow one of the laptops from here?"

"Be my guest," Kate said. "You've got a paycheck on your desk, so technically you're still employed. But do me a favor. Look for any other explanation. Something isn't right about this. Vince is crazy about your mom. He always has been. Just give him the benefit of the doubt until you can prove otherwise."

I wasn't sure what to think when she said Vince had always been crazy about my mom. Like *always* always, or since my dad died always? But she distracted me with her next statement.

"Maybe he's working on something," Kate said.

"He's retired," I said automatically. And then I thought about what my mother had said about him going through my dad's old boxes.

"Cops never retire," she said. "Not really. They just stop putting on the uniform."

Retirement had been hard on my dad. He'd loved being a cop more than anything in the world. I'd never realized until his retirement how much he hadn't been there through my childhood. When he wasn't on shift, he was working off-duty details or doing surveillance. He lived and breathed police work, to the detriment of everything else.

As a child, I hadn't realized what it had done to my mother. And as much as Aunt Scarlet liked to think I was a chip off the old block on the Holmes side of the family, I realized I had a lot of my own mother in me too. My dad had been a cop at work and at home, and the mother I knew in my childhood was not the mother I knew now.

She'd been a buttoned-up accountant and so uptight I wasn't sure how she kept from popping. At least that's how she'd been around my dad. But Phoebe and I had gotten glimpses of a wild and creative woman beneath the shoulder pads and pantyhose when it was just us and she was able to let her hair down a little. But when my dad was around, or she thought he might be coming home from shift, she made sure the house was spotless and that we were out of his hair so he could rest.

I think my mother only started to discover herself after my father died. Or maybe she'd known all along and just chosen to keep it hidden because she knew he wouldn't like it. My father was a hard man—a straight arrow and a rule follower. Everyone always said that's what made him a good cop. As his daughter, I had mixed feelings on the subject. He did have a dry sense of humor I enjoyed, and we didn't really bond until his retirement, but only when there was a game on.

I don't remember ever having any heart-to-hearts with my father. My mother took care of the milestones in a teenage girl's life for both me and my sister. But I was always the luckier of the two of us. Phoebe was five years younger than me, and he wanted even less to do with her. Phoebe had taken his wishes to heart, and she'd escaped from Whiskey Bayou minutes after graduating from high school. She hadn't come back until his funeral.

I could understand what Kate meant when she said they didn't stop being cops just because they hung up the uniform. After my dad's retirement, he was either in his office poring over old case files or sitting in front of the TV watching sports.

"Maybe you're right," I said, getting to my feet.

"Can I talk now?" Scarlet asked, unlocking her mouth key.

"You just did," I said.

"Huh," she said. "How about that? Those keys are tricky."

Kate smiled and sat up. "So what are you going to do?"

"I'm going to see what I can find out," I said.

"That's all I can do. The priority is finding Vince. He's been gone two days."

"She could file a missing persons," Kate said.

"I think she'd rather die than do that," I said. "I don't think Mom would be too keen on letting the whole police department her new husband was gone. I just need to find him and bring him back. Once that's done they can work it out between themselves. I'm going to check Dad's office and the shed behind the house to see if I can find any clues to where he's gone. But not today. I'm going to grab a laptop and then Scarlet and I going home. I'm stick-a-fork-in-me done."

"That makes me think of chicken-fried steak," Scarlet said. "Maybe we could have chicken-fried steak with white gravy for dinner. And mashed potatoes."

"Anything else?" I asked.

"That ought to do it," she said, and walked out of the room.

"That does sound good," I said.

"Maybe eat a vegetable so you don't give birth to one of those twenty-pound babies," Kate said, grabbing one of the afghans from the back of the chair and lying back down. "Do you know what a twenty-pound baby would do to your vagina?"

"I can't imagine it's good," I said, crossing my legs.

"Turn the light off on your way out."

When Scarlet and I got back to the house, she hit the bar in the butler's pantry, made herself a drink, and then gave me an absent wave and then headed straight to her room.

I was feeling a little exhausted myself, but I was still hopped up on sugar, so while my body was tired, my mind was going full speed. I changed out of my bumblebee attire into what I liked to call my work-from-home outfit, which was essentially anything that felt like pajamas, but was still nice enough you could answer the door if someone showed up unexpectedly.

After I was suitably attired, I decided a sandwich was in order. I added lettuce and tomato because the thought of having a twenty-pound baby was terrifying, and then I grabbed a bottle of water to wash away the caffeine.

It wasn't long before I heard the rumbling sounds of Scarlet's snores. I turned on the evening news to drown her out, and it was just good luck that Nick's homicide was the breaking story. It was nice to catch a glimpse of him as he told the reporter no information at all, while making them think he was giving important information. It helped that the reporter was a woman and she seemed dazzled by his presence.

Nick was a fantastic cop, but the department had made him somewhat of a spokesman over the last few years because he was just as good in the public eye as he was behind crime scene tape. He was sexy as hell, he had charisma, and people liked him. He'd do well in politics.

Ever since Nick had given me the greenlight on doing some redecorating, my mind had been going nonstop. I'd been having trouble lately focusing. I had two pages of notes, and a fresh new Pinterest board. Now I just had to find someone who could get it all done. Because cop hours and pregnant ladies weren't conducive to home remodeling. Especially if you wanted to finish the project.

I sent out a feeler to Suzanne since she'd been in the construction business once upon a time. I'd read about nesting, but I hadn't expected the urge to redecorate the entire house to come on so strong. I wanted it done yesterday.

I brought my sandwich to the kitchen table where I'd set up the agency laptop, my notes, and all the information my mother had given me. I needed to pay another visit to my mother and check out my dad's shed, but there was no use doing it in the dark and rain. Tomorrow morning would be soon enough.

It felt strange running a background check on Vince, but I figured it was best to follow protocol and treat this just like I would any other case. I started running the search, and then I opened another tab so I could do the reverse phone lookup and find out who Angelica was.

"Luis Vega," I said, writing the name down on my notepad. "Of course it's not going to be easy."

Now I had to do a search for Luis Vega and work my way backward until I found someone named Angelica. While I waited for the computer, I flipped back and forth between Pinterest and HGTV and sent pictures to Suzanne and Rosemarie. Suzanne assured me she had a crew who could start immediately and just to send pictures and they'd take care of the rest.

I liked the idea of someone else taking care of everything. I wanted a no-stress pregnancy, and I wanted Nick to have as little of a headache as possible. As long as he kept getting called out to murders, I'd be in the clear.

Vince's background check finished first and I pulled up the file. I skimmed over the standard information—driver's license, social security number, photo ID—and wanted to get to the nitty gritty of his past. People didn't realize that even their social media information showed up on background checks now days. It was impossible to hide something if you used technology.

I didn't really know anything about Vince's past, even though he'd been around since before my sister Phoebe was born. Vince had been married to a woman named Margaret Dixon Walker from Charleston for about two years before she'd filed for divorce and they'd gone their separate ways. No children. And he had no other marriages or long-term relationships until he'd married my mother a couple of years ago.

I thought it strange for a man to go that long without a serious relationship, but it looked like he'd been married to his career. He'd been highly decorated as an officer and there were several articles I found about him and my father and a couple of high-profile cases and task forces they'd been a part of.

All in all, there were no obvious skeletons in Vince's closet. His ex-wife had been remarried for twenty years and had two grown children with her second husband. Vince paid his taxes, and he didn't have outstanding amounts of debt.

Now, I only had to find out who Luis Vega was and why Vince had his phone number in his pocket.

It wasn't hard to find Angelica's name in the list of known acquaintances or family members. Angelica Vega. Wife to Luis.

And within seconds I had an address to go with the phone number. It looked like I'd be taking a trip to Miami.

CHAPTER SIX

"IS SOMEONE MOWING THE LAWN?" NICK ASKED sleepily. "It's the middle of the night."

I vaguely remembered him getting in the bed at some point and pulling me into his arms. I'd been in a deep sleep and having very good dreams when he'd woken me up with his question.

"It's Scarlet," I mumbled. "She's in the guest room."

Nick sighed and spooned close to me again, and then put the pillow over his head. "I must've been really tired when I came in to have not heard that."

"Think of it as white noise," I said.

He laughed and then threw back the covers, and I pulled them back over my head. When he came back sometime later he was showered and dressed, and he sat on the side of the bed.

"I've got to go back into the station anyway," he said, leaning down to kiss me. "Sleep is overrated."

"Speak for yourself," I said. "Next time you get to carry the baby."

"Next time?" he asked. The bed shook with his laughter. "What do you have planned for our future, Mrs. Dempsey?"

"Don't call me that," I said, creaking my eyes open. "Whenever you call me that, I keep expecting your mother to pop around the corner. That kind of anxiety isn't good for the baby."

He laughed even harder.

"I've got lots of stuff planned for our future," I said, smiling back. "You're going to love it."

"We'll see," he said. "But I love you, so that's good enough. Give me a call once you stop throwing up."

"Don't remind me," I said, pulling the covers over my head.

A few minutes later I decided Nick had cursed me, and I was running to the bathroom. I'd learned a lot about bathrooms over the last few weeks, and it was worth noting that good bathmats were a necessity. The ones in Nick's bathroom felt like tiny mattresses, and I was very comfortable all things considered.

Once the nausea passed, I crawled into the shower and let the water bring me back to life. I might have fallen asleep a little, but the buzz of my phone snapped me to attention. I hadn't realized I'd brought it into the shower with me and set it on the built-in shelf.

It was Rosemarie, and I debated whether or not

to answer it, but I knew if I didn't she'd just keep calling.

"Hello," I croaked.

"Yikes," she said. "Did you get possessed during the night?"

"I don't think so, but I'm past the point of ruling anything out," I said. "I'm just doing my ritualistic communing with the toilet bowl."

"What you need is a surprise," Rosemarie said.

"Really?" I asked. "Because I was thinking what I needed was to go back to bed and sleep this off."

"It's 'cause you're not eating healthy," she said. "The healthier you eat, the less morning sickness you'll have."

"How do you know that?" I asked. "And why didn't you tell me sooner?"

"I saw it on *Good Morning Savannah*," she said. "I figured you'd know what you were doing. You seem like the kind of woman who has it all together."

"Have you been paying attention as we've been hanging out over the last couple of years?" I asked, cocking my head to the side. I thought that was rather presumptuous of her considering she'd witnessed me *not* having it together on more than one occasion.

Rosemarie just stayed silent.

"I've never been pregnant before," I said. "I don't know anything."

"You should get one of those books," Rosemarie said. "I hear they're real helpful. Giving birth can't be that hard. If cavewomen used to do it while running from dinosaurs I figure yours should be a walk in the park."

"I guess when you put it that way." I turned the water off and grabbed the towel I'd laid over the warming rod, and I moaned as I wrapped it around my sore body. "So what's the surprise?" I asked, barely bothering to dry off as I stumbled back toward the bed.

"We're outside!" she said. "Come open the door. The rain is gone. It's a beautiful day, and you're going to love this. I promise."

"How can it be a beautiful day?" I asked. "It's barely seven o'clock in the morning." I looked out the picture window in the bedroom and saw the sun shining through the trees.

"We haven't had sun in weeks," Rosemarie said. "I'd almost forgotten what it looked like. It's still colder than Nina Dempsey's heart out here, but we're well on the way to spring. But maybe you could come open the front door and let us in because I didn't wear a coat on account of I didn't want it to interfere with my outfit."

"Us?" I asked, grabbing my robe from the foot of the bed.

"That's part of the surprise," Rosemarie said.

I could hear the excitement in her voice, and I knew whatever was going on was bound to be a disaster. I blew out a breath. "I'll be there in a minute."

Scarlet was still snoring, so I took that as a good sign. I could only handle crazy in small doses.

The sunlight was blinding as I walked to the front of the house, the wood floors streaked with dappled light. My steps slowed as I got a glimpse of Rosemarie standing with a group of men through the window, and I almost didn't open the door, but she saw me.

"Hey," I said, looking her over. She wore denim overalls and a long-sleeved flannel shirt, and her Farrah Fawcett hair was tied into pigtails. She had a tool belt and a clipboard.

There were several men surrounding her, of various shapes and sizes, but I noticed immediately that they were all in very good shape. Like, very good shape. These were some of the most beautiful men I'd ever seen. I was not going to be happy if my surprise was a bunch of strippers.

"Wha—what's going on here?" I asked, taking a step back.

"This is your surprise," Rosemarie said, practically bouncing out of her Doc Martens.

"I'm definitely surprised," I said. "I just don't know what I'm surprised about."

Rosemarie came inside the house and the men followed behind her. It was then I noticed they all had tool belts and sledgehammers, and I started to get a sinking feeling in my gut.

"She looks like she might pass out," a familiar voice said. "You'd better sit her down. I'll get some water."

"Suzanne?" I asked, as Rosemarie took me by the arm and led me to the orgy couch. That's the only way I could think of it now since Scarlet's declaration that it reminded her of one.

"I'm Barry today," he said. "This kind of work needs an Adam's apple."

He brought me a bottle of water and then looked around the house, nodding casually and muttering under his breath. He was a stunning woman, but he was also a very attractive man. His head was bald as a billiard, and he was muscular with broad shoulders and narrow hips. He wasn't wearing the silicone boobs today or the corset, so it was like meeting him for the first time.

"You look like Idris Elba," I said. "But without hair."

"I get that a lot," he said. "And it's easier to put on the wigs without the hair. That's a little tip of the trade."

"Don't tell Scarlet," I said.

"This house has good bones," Barry said. "All you need is a meshing of styles. It's real easy to see what Nick's style is since this was his place. He likes simple, clean lines and modern furniture. But your style is about as opposite from that as you can get if your Pinterest board is anything to go by. I stayed up late last night going through the photos, and I've been working up a design scheme. Richard here is an architect, so he can help us with load-bearing walls and all that technical stuff. Now get that panicked look off your face. You're just going to have to trust me. We're going to go with modern rustic. It's very chic right now."

"Why? How? Who?" I asked, apparently unable to form complete sentences.

"Oh, that's easy," Rosemarie said. "This is what friends are for. You've got a rogue husband to find and a baby on the way. Look at this as a really expensive shower gift, only you're going to have to pay us instead of the other way around, and it'll take a lot longer than one afternoon."

"Nick is going to kill me," I said.

"Pssh," Barry said. "You are carrying his child. That man would give you the moon right now if he could. Take advantage of this while you can because after your childbearing years I hear you have to manipulate and go behind his back."

"What about your businesses?" I asked. "You can't just close up shop to do this. Whatever this..." I said, waving my hand, "...is. It's nuts."

"That's why I put my old crew back together," Barry said. "This is Lonny, Brandon, Carlos, and Richard. They do good work. As far as me and Rosemarie, you let us worry about our schedules. She's appointment only, and I have employees just for this reason."

"You do a lot of random renovations for almost strangers?" I asked.

Barry laughed, and that was a very familiar sound. "I've got occupational ADD. It comes from growing up rich and becoming bored easily. I just like to keep myself entertained while I'm spending my trust fund."

"But the cake shop," I said. "You're so talented."

"I didn't say I wasn't talented, but the cake shop just started turning a profit this year. I love making cakes. But when I don't feel like doing it I don't. I'm in high demand. And if I can confess, it pisses my mother off when she sees me driving the van around town."

"It's all a web of lies," I said, shaking my head.

"What's going on here?" Scarlet said from the stairs. "I could hear the ruckus all the way in my bedroom. I was getting my beauty sleep."

Everyone stood frozen for a moment at the sight of her. She wore a leopard-print silk robe with a fur collar, her hair was in a turban, and mascara was smudged under her eyes so she looked like she'd been in a fight and lost. If Cruella de Vil had a much older and shorter sister, it would've been Scarlet.

"Sorry about that, Scarlet," Rosemarie said, a little too cheerfully. "We came over with a surprise for Addison."

Scarlet looked each of the men over like she was buying a horse at auction. "Ooh, I love a good strip show," she said, rubbing her hands together. "Did I miss it? Let me get my dollars. I keep them in an envelope under the mattress just in case."

Richard looked at Barry. "She has stripper emergencies?"

"Don't ask," Barry said.

Scarlet turned to go back upstairs but I stopped her. "They're not strippers," I told her. "They're construction workers."

"I don't think so," she said. "I know a stripper when I see one. That one there has shaved legs."

"Laser hair removal," Carlos said. "I've got a show tonight, and shaving this much body hair is a real bitch."

I could appreciate that sentiment.

"What kind of a show?" Scarlet asked. "I like a good show. You got extra tickets?"

Carlos smiled. "I've got a front table just for you."

"Carlos does a mean Liza Minnelli," Barry said.

"Huh," Scarlet said, looking at Barry. And then she narrowed her eyes. "Do I know you?"

"I'm Suzanne. From the cake shop," Barry said.

"Oh, good," she said, as recognition came into her eyes. "I thought maybe you were one of my walk of shames." She blew out a sigh of relief. "I've had a few over the years. And you're just my type. It's real awkward when you run into them after you sneak out into the night."

"I've been there," Barry said. "It's not our fault. We're just too beautiful, and people get so attached."

"Did you bring breakfast?" Scarlet asked.

"It's in my trunk," he said.

"You might be husband number six if you keep romancing me like this."

Barry threw his head back and laughed. I was glad everyone was having a great time, acting like they weren't seconds away from knocking the house down. Not to mention this didn't exactly jive with my plans.

My plans for the day had included going back to my mother's and catching a flight to Miami. Nowhere in my plans was having my house demolished by drag queens or dragging Scarlet along with me to keep her out of trouble and rubble. I could get things done more efficiently if I left my two sidekicks at home. And I could be twice as efficient if I could talk Nick into making a quick trip with me. People listened to Nick. They stopped when he told them to stop. No one chased him with knives or Weed eaters. I felt bad about asking him, but there was a chance he'd wrapped his case. It was a small chance, but a chance is a chance.

I thought through my plan of action, and I figured the only way I could do it without hurting anyone's feelings was to lie or manipulate. Or maybe a little of both.

I pulled Rosemarie to the side while Barry made himself at home and toured the house with the crew. It felt like this was one of those times where I should just go with whatever they had planned, so that's what I was going to do. I was going to have complete faith in my friends to make sure that my baby had a place to come home to that wasn't a construction site six and a half months from now. Because if not, I wasn't even ashamed to say that I would hunt down and torture every last one of them and dance on their corpses while holding my swaddled baby.

"I have a favor to ask," I said to Rosemarie, dropping my voice to a whisper. "I need to go to my mother's and work on a few things regarding the case, but I don't want to bring Scarlet with me because I don't want anyone to die. My mother took knife-throwing lessons a few months ago, and it turns out she's really good at it."

Rosemarie nodded conspiratorially. "I understand just what you're saying," she said. "I guess Scarlet and Phyllis do rub each other the wrong way. Leave her here with me. I'll make sure she doesn't get into any trouble."

"I'd appreciate it," I said, patting her on the back.

Rosemarie went off to join Barry, and Scarlet came into the kitchen a few minutes later to start a pot of coffee. I closed my eyes and let the smell of dark roast wash over me. I missed coffee. I figured if I drank something that kept me awake and made me miserable when I went too long without, it probably had the same effects on the baby. Since tea made me calm and put me to sleep, I was hoping the same theory applied.

Scarlet was still wearing her robe and turban, but she'd added red lipstick somewhere along the way. I didn't know if it was for appearances' sake or because she really thought Barry was romancing her.

"I have a favor to ask," I said.

"I'm not much on favors," she said, staring at the coffeepot as if that would make it brew faster. "If I do you a favor, then everyone is going to want a favor. And then you're going to owe me a favor. Last time I did somebody a favor they up and died on me before I could collect. Then I had to steal a pocket watch off a man at a wake."

My mouth dropped open and I was momentarily speechless. "Don't think of it as a favor then," I said, once my wits came back. "Think of it as being in charge."

She perked up at that. "I like being in charge. What do you have in mind?"

"These guys are here to do some home renovations," I said. "I'm not exactly sure how things got to this point, but they escalated quickly. I have no idea what they plan to do or how extensive the work is going to be."

She nodded thoughtfully. "I get it. You want to make sure they don't screw up." She pursed her lips and finally removed the pot and stuck her cup directly under where the coffee was coming out. "I've seen Rosemarie's place. She's got questionable taste. I've never seen a gingham and leather combo before."

I winced. "That pretty much describes Rosemarie perfectly. I'd appreciate you being a project manager of sorts while I'm gone. It's not a favor. It's a job."

"And I'm the boss," she said, nodding. "You can count on me. I wonder if they have an extra hard hat. I saw one on Amazon that looks like a pink cowboy hat. I'm going to go one-click that bad boy.

By the time they get done with this place it'll look like a million bucks."

"I'm pretty sure it already looks like a million bucks. Plus some." And I hoped to God Nick had been serious when he'd told me it was okay to make the house my own, because we were about to get past the point of no return.

"I might be gone overnight," I said. "I've got some work to do today to find Vince."

"It's probably best," she told me. "Jobs like this always look worse before they look better. Besides, if you don't find that husband of your mother's she's going to be insufferable. Phyllis always does better with a man. Maybe one of these guys is available."

I smiled tightly and decided the sooner I got out of there the better. I thanked her again and then ran upstairs. I got dressed in leggings and an oversized angora sweater in army green. I put on matching booties and a wide black leather belt and decided that was a much better choice than the day before's bumblebee faux pas. It wouldn't be long before I was too big for anything cute.

I was due in September, which wasn't quite as hot as August, but it was still ranked in heat somewhere between the devil's underwear and the metal slides at the park when I was a kid.

I packed a small overnight bag, and then I put the laptop and all of my files into my knockoff Louis Vuitton tote that I'd bought out of someone's trunk on River Street near the Talmadge Bridge, grabbed my keys and jacket, and headed to the door. I was getting a much later start than I'd planned.

"Have a good trip," Barry said, appearing from somewhere in the house.

I winced. I wasn't sure dragging my mother's husband home in disgrace would qualify as a good trip.

"Can you do me a favor?" I asked.

"There's a lot of that going around lately," he said, raising a brow at me.

My cheeks flushed with guilt and I coughed delicately. "I've got to call Nick and tell him about all of...this. It's a lot to take in. Just do me a favor and go slow. Maybe a room at a time. Or just not too much mess. He doesn't do change well."

Barry shrugged. "He's a man. We're resistant. But I can dig it."

I waved goodbye and headed to the garage. I'd decided the Audi wasn't going to cut it today. Sometimes a girl had to go big, and Black Betty was just what I needed. I decided to call Nick and get the hard part over with. And the good news was I'd already packed a bag if he kicked me out.

The phone only rang once before he picked up.

"Are you naked?" Nick asked.

"That would be awkward," I said. "Especially on these leather seats."

"Leather," he said. "That's sexy. Tell me where you are. I can be there in ten minutes."

I snorted out a laugh. "I'm running errands. And I need to visit my mother."

"And...you killed it," he said with a sigh. "Do you think we'll ever get to have sex again?"

"It's only been two days."

"That's something a married woman would say. You never would've said that while we were just shacking up."

I could usually tell what kind of day Nick was having by his level of sarcasm. Dealing with murder and the casually wasted lives of human beings was never easy, and I knew from dealing with my father that every cop handled it differently.

"You're running errands before nine o'clock in the morning?" he asked.

"It's a long story."

"Why are you going to your mother's?"

I turned right out of our driveway and headed toward Savannah. I'd told Nick I was doing errands, which I was, but my mother's house wasn't my first stop. I'd been putting off seeing Savage since I'd been back from our honeymoon. Savage had been shot at my wedding going after a criminal priest, and we'd delayed leaving for our honeymoon until Savage was out of the woods and on his way to a full recovery.

He was my friend, and I felt bad about not stopping by to check on him after we'd gotten back from Tahiti. Maybe it was awkward because he'd had feelings for me at some point. Or maybe it was awkward because I was married now and that put our friendship in limbo, especially since he'd taken a promotion to head up the South Dakota field office.

I didn't know where we stood, but that didn't mean I couldn't take him a fruit basket and pay him a visit.

"Hello? Addison?" Nick asked.

"Sorry," I said. "I zoned out. I want to check out my dad's old shed behind the house before I go any farther looking for Vince. Mom said Vince had been spending a lot of time out there lately, and she also said that's where Dad's old case files were kept."

"Let me know if you find anything promising," he said. "I can always check on things from my end. See if he was talking to anyone or if anyone knows anything. Vince hasn't been retired that long. Only a few years. So he's still got a lot of friends on the force."

"I'll remember that," I said. "Honestly, I just want to get this over and done with. I feel kind of skeezy after digging around in his past last night. I don't mind doing it on strangers, but it's weird when it's someone you know."

"You've never run a background check on me?" Nick asked.

"Well," I said, cornered. "That doesn't count. It was early in our relationship. You can't be too careful as a single woman in this world. There are all kinds of creepers out there. What if you'd been married? Or a pervert? Fortunately, you passed the test."

Nick barked out a laugh. "I'm glad to know I made the cut."

"You know how happy you are to hear my voice right now?" I asked.

"This should be good," he said.

"I just want you to remember that happiness as I proceed with the conversation."

"Again," he said. "This should be good."

"This is important," I said. The gravity in my voice must have put him on alert.

"If it's that important I can take some personal time and meet you somewhere," he said. "Is something wrong? Is it the baby?"

"No, nothing like that," I assured him. "Honestly, I'd rather have this conversation on the phone. Don't be mad."

"Okay," he said. "But we're not naming the baby Scarlet. No matter how much she said she'd pay you."

"Funny," I said. "Though we should probably circle back around to that conversation at another time. No, this has to do with Vince and how Mom asked me to bring him back so she could kill him."

"I don't recall you mentioning anything about how she was going to kill him."

"I might have let that part slip my mind when I was filling you in," I said. "And there's a good chance she was only kidding anyway."

"I'm glad she has limits," he said.

"Not many, but they're there on occasion," I told him. "Anyway, I know you're wanting me to take it easy because of the baby, and technically, I'm not really working for the agency anymore, so it shouldn't even count as a case."

"But you agreed to do whatever it is you need to do to find Vince," Nick said, guessing where I was going.

"Right," I said.

"That's understandable," he said. "She's your mother."

"I'm glad you said that," I said. "Because I need to go to Miami.".

"Wait...what?" he asked. "What's in Miami?"

"The woman whose number was in Vince's pants pocket," I said. "Her name is Angelica Vega. Maybe Vince is there with her. And if not, I want to talk to her. Obviously, she knows Vince. I just hate leaving Mom in the dark. I know the half of her that doesn't want to kill Vince is really worried about him."

Nick sighed. I was a trial at times. "I know you're going to go anyway," he said. "But do me a favor? Take Kate instead of Scarlet or Rosemarie."

"I was actually going to ask you to go with me," I said. "I'm not a complete dummy."

"I never thought you were," he said. "And I actually would go if I wasn't up to my eyeballs in dismembered body parts. But Kate's the next best thing. I know she won't let anything happen to you."

"Dismembered body parts?" I asked. "The news didn't mention anything about that last night."

"They will tonight," he said. "We thought it

was a pretty cut-and-dry case. Your standard domestic dispute. Husband and wife take their argument to the front yard so the neighbors have courtside seats. Wife pulls gun on husband. Husband pulls shotgun on wife. And then they shoot each other."

"How does that involve dismemberment?" I asked.

"We checked their freezer."

"Yikes," I said. "At least no one is shooting at you."

"Not today," he said.

"Which leads me to the second part of the conversation I'd like you to not get mad about," I said.

I heard a *thunk*. "What was that?"

"My head hitting the steering wheel," he said. "When you said you had something important to talk about I pulled off the road as a safety precaution."

"That's very conscientious of you," I said. "How long do you think you'll be working on this case?"

"Until we figure out who all the body parts in the freezer belong to," he said. "Why?"

"So that could take weeks?"

"Maybe. Why?" he asked again.

Now it was my turn to sigh. "I was just thinking it might be a good idea to stay busy for a few weeks."

"This is Savannah. Staying busy has never been an issue. Especially for a homicide detective. You realize I'm going to keep asking why until you tell me, right?"

"Remember how you told me I could do some renovating? And that it was my house too and you wanted me to feel at home."

"Uh-oh," he said.

"Yeah, about that." I paused, trying to think of the best way to phrase it. But there really wasn't a best way, so I just went for it. "You see, Suzanne used to be a contractor."

"Wait a second," he said. "The cross-dressing cake baker, Suzanne?"

"Yeah, that's the one," I confirmed. "And she and Rosemarie and Scarlet took my ideas and a whole bunch of Pinterest pictures and came up with a plan. And Suzanne brought her construction crew."

"They're doing construction?" Nick asked. "Like tearing down walls?"

"Yeah, but it's going to be great," I said. *Eventually. Probably.* "It'll be modern rustic, so it combines both of our styles."

"Sounds expensive," he said.

"It's probably on the higher end of the budget."

"Do I have any alternatives?" he asked.

"There's a house for sale on your parents' street that's just been renovated," I said. "We could buy it and be their neighbors."

"Point taken," he said. "Love you. And tell me when you get to Miami so I know you're safe."

"It's just Miami," I said. "What could go wrong?"

CHAPTER SEVEN

SAVAGE WAS ONE OF THOSE MEN WHO WAS ALMOST unexplainable. His body was a temple, his muscles had muscles, his face was like carved granite, and he had the sun-kissed skin and high cheekbones of his Native American ancestors. He was a god among men, and boy, did he know it.

Back when I'd first started at the agency, Savage had recommended a house in an older, well-kept neighborhood that was almost in my price range. I hadn't realized at the time that Savage lived in the house across the street. Having Savage for a neighbor had been interesting, especially when my hormones hadn't completely been committed to Nick.

I turned onto the familiar street and knew every eye in the neighborhood was on me. I'd never experienced anything like it—not even in Whiskey Bayou, where spying on your neighbor could've been an Olympic event. But the neighborhood watch—or

NAD Squad as they liked to call themselves—was a cut above the rest. NAD Squad stood for Neighbors Against Delinquency. I'm not sure if the criminals stayed away from this street because everyone was bonkers, or because of the vigilance of the watch.

I'd bought the cute little dark blue house with white trim from a friend of Savage's once my bank account had become more flush from successful PI work. It was right across the street from Savage's, and when I moved out, I'd let my sister move in while she was in transition. Since Phoebe tended to be in transition a lot, I wasn't surprised when she'd moved back out after a couple of months.

My relationship with Nick had been somewhat volatile before we'd both decided to commit, so I hadn't rented the house again, and I hadn't put it on the market to sell. I'd kind of forgotten all about it with everything that had been going on the last month. I made a mental note to get in touch with a realtor.

But as soon as I had the thought I wondered if maybe I hadn't sold the house because I was psychic. Maybe my subconscious knew that Rosemarie and Suzanne would be demolishing my house and Nick and I would need a place to stay if things got too bad.

I decided to run the prospect by him, and make sure everything inside was in good shape. I was one of those people who liked to have a plan and a backup plan. I made lists for my lists. And color coordinating my calendar was one of my favorite things to do. We could treat it like a honeymoon cottage. Or at least that was how I was going to sell him on the idea.

I parked street side since Savage's Tahoe was in the driveway. I was surprised to see there were no other cars. Nick and I had spent quite a bit of time at the hospital those first few days, and it seemed like there was always someone there. He had parents and sisters and assorted aunts, uncles, and cousins. He'd been well cared for, and it had been weird to see a man who seemed like a loner have a big, boisterous family. It made me wonder what other hidden facets there were to Savage.

I got the giant gift basket from the back seat, and when I turned around, Savage was standing at the door. He wore gray sweatpants that rode low on his hips and a white T-shirt that clung to the impressive muscles in his arms and chest. I could see the bulge of bandages through his shirt, and I wondered if he was supposed to be up and moving around like he was.

"I was wondering when you were going to stop by for a visit," he said, pushing open the screen door.

My feet were glued to where I stood. I'd forgotten how powerful and magnetic Savage's presence was. He grinned as if he knew what I was thinking and was daring me to come inside.

"Yeah, I was wondering that too," Mr. Walner yelled from across the street. He was dressed in a maroon robe and leaned on his walker, shaking a newspaper up in the air. "I read about you in the paper. Now you're highfalutin, living up in your mansion. They had pictures of your wedding in the Savannah paper. Said you invited the whole town."

Guilt swamped me. I hadn't even thought about extending invitations to anyone in the neighborhood. The wedding had been such a cluster I couldn't even imagine adding them to the mix.

"I think the news coverage had more to do with Savage getting shot than my marriage," I called out.

He *hmmph*ed and his screen door slammed shut as he went back inside, but I could still see him watching us at the window.

"You married a rich city boy instead of one of your own kind," another voice called out. I turned to look at the house next door to mine and saw Leonard Winkle standing on his stoop in what looked like a Chewbacca onesie.

"Hi, Spock," I said. "One of my own kind?"

"From the neighborhood," he said. "We stick together here. NAD Squad forever." He made some kind of complicated hand gesture and finished it up with a peace sign.

Since the NAD Squad had consisted of twenty-something fantasy nerds, Mrs. Rodriguez, a computer geek, a hermit, and Savage, the potential for marrying within the neighborhood seemed like slim pickins.

On the surface, Savage probably seemed like a respectable choice, but he'd been a no-no from the start for me. There were some men you just knew would be bad for you, and Savage was that man for me. He was a great guy, and the sex would've been amazing, but Savage and I would've eventually imploded. And no matter how much he liked the pursuit, I didn't see Savage as the marrying kind. Nick was my perfect balance to the insanity of my life. Savage only fueled the fire.

"It's good to see you, Spock," I said.

"You too," he said, grinning. "I'm having a get-together later if you want to drop by. I'm making my famous pimento cheese dip and we're doing *Harry Potter* charades."

"I would if I could, but I'm heading out of town," I said.

"Maybe next time," he said.

I looked up and down the street. Several of my former neighbors stood on the porches, staring blatantly, scowls of disapproval on their faces. Their judgement was thick in the air.

I noticed the *For Sale* sign in Savage's yard, and it reminded me that his days on the block were numbered as well. A pang of sadness that I hadn't been expecting hit me square in the chest. I thought about where we'd started and how much we'd changed during our relationship.

I blinked rapidly to dry my eyes, and I carried the gift basket up to the front door, ignoring the stares.

"I can't decide if they're mad at me or you," I said.

"A little of both," he said, grinning. "Ever since

the *For Sale* sign went up in the yard Mrs. Rodriguez has been doing the voodoo on me pretty regularly"

"Yikes," I said. "Seems kind of harsh for a man who's just been shot."

"She's hardcore," Savage said.

"Any offers on the house?" I asked, looking around.

I'd never actually been in Savage's house before. I always figured if I crossed the threshold that it would be the point of no return. He had moving boxes stacked and neatly labeled—which I appreciated—and his furniture consisted of a beige couch and a leather recliner that looked well used. There was nothing left on the wall, and no personal touches of anything lying around that I could see.

"Just got one this morning," he said. "We'll see if it pans out. Is that for me?"

"I know how your body is a temple, so I got you a fruit basket. But just in case you've let things go to hell the last few weeks, there are chocolate bars hidden under the fruit."

"You got those for you, didn't you?" he asked.

"I wouldn't turn one down if you wanted to share."

"Come on in," he said, shutting the front door behind me. "You want coffee?"

"No, I'm off coffee," I said. "It's not good for the...baby," I finished softly.

"I've got water," he said, smoothly.

"Thanks, I appreciate it," I said, realizing I was still holding the basket in front of me like a shield.

"Just put it in here," he said, pointing to the tiny kitchen island.

The farther I walked into the house, the more it felt like I was walking into the lion's den. I put the basket down and took the bottled water, chugging half of it quickly.

"So you're really doing it," I said. "Really moving."

"Yeah, I've got a couple more weeks of PT before my doctors will release me, but after that I'm free to go. I'll send you a postcard once I get there."

"Where is there?" I asked.

"I found a house in a town called Normal."

I burst out laughing. "You're kidding," I said. "That's like inviting karma to be your roommate."

He shrugged. "It definitely has its quirks. But it's the Wild West up there. People are using the local Indian reservations as body dumping grounds, which means it falls under the jurisdiction of Bureau of Indian Affairs. But they don't have the resources or manpower the FBI does, so I'm the bridge between the two agencies."

"You think it's a serial killer?" I asked, intrigued.

"No," he said. "Drugs and trafficking for the most part. It's wide-open land."

"I always forget how depressing your job is," I said.

"Believe me, working with you and the agency is my downtime," he said.

My smile was pressed tight. People didn't realize how men like Nick and Savage suffered in their jobs. But if somebody like them didn't do it, who would?

"It looks like you're moving around better," I said. "You definitely look better than the last time I saw you. Pale is not a good color on you."

He smiled and pulled out a barstool for me to sit down at the tiny island in his kitchen. I didn't know what to do with my hands, and words kept tumbling from my mouth.

"I saw your *For Sale* sign and remembered I should probably put the house across the street on the market."

"I figured you were keeping it for your escape hatch," he said.

"Escape hatch?"

"Yeah, for the next time you freak out about being married and having a baby on the way," he said. "You've got commitment issues."

"No I don't," I said, squenching my face in shock.

"That's what you do," Savage said. "You have a fight. You panic. You move to a new location. You have an existential crisis. You panic. You move to a new location. I figured you'd be back on the block eventually. I figure getting abandoned at the altar did more damage than you let on."

"What are you, a psychologist now? I do not have commitment issues," I said, feeling the heat flush my face. "You have commitment issues." I knew it was a lame comeback, but he was putting doubt in my mind. Did I really have commitment issues?

"It's not commitment issues if you don't want to be committed," he said.

"Aha!" I said, pointing a finger. "I knew that I would just be another notch in your bedpost. A...a one-night booty call. A bang buddy. A wham-bam-thank-you-ma'am. I ain't no hollaback girl."

Savage was doubled over with laughter, holding his chest where he'd been shot, and tears were streaming out of his eyes.

"Lord, are you trying to kill me?" he asked. "I had a feeling you'd be the death of me."

He was looking a little pale, and then I started to worry that maybe he was dying. "Maybe you should sit down," I said, taking his arm and trying to haul him over to the recliner. That worked about as well as trying to move a semi.

"And just for the record," he said. "I would've committed to you. I think you ruined me for all other women." He grinned when I let go of his arm like I was touching something hot. "Do I make you nervous?"

"Of course not," I said. I could've really used one of those candy bars hiding under the fruit. Savage must've read my mind because he flicked open his pocketknife and sliced right through the cellophane. I grabbed a Snickers and tore it open.

"We can still be friends, you know. It doesn't have to be weird."

I felt the tears prick my eyes and blinked them

back, staring at the half-eaten candy bar. "It doesn't have to be," I said. "But it is. And I hate it. We had feelings for each other, no matter what kind of feelings they were. Friendship was part of that, but there were more intimate feelings for a time." I sighed and finally found the courage to look him in the eyes. "So yeah, I went back and forth on whether or not to come see you at all."

His eyes were dark and intense, and in them was understanding and something else...love. "I know you and Nick were both there in the hospital," he said. "For days. My family told me. Thank you for that. Thank you both."

My smile wobbled. "That's what friends do. You're a good man, Savage. *And* a good friend. You're going to meet your match one day. I don't doubt it. The women in Normal, South Dakota, won't know what hit them."

"Ha," he said, his eyes squinting with laughter. "Normal is a town of just a couple thousand people. I wouldn't bank on it."

"I need to take off," I said, crumpling the empty wrapper in my hand. "I'm working a missing persons case."

He raised his brows at that. "I thought you were done with PI work? Who's missing?"

"Vince Walker," I said. "My mother's husband. She thinks he ran off with another woman."

"What do you think?" he asked.

"I think I have unanswered questions that I need to get to the bottom of."

CHAPTER EIGHT

BY THE TIME I LEFT SAVAGE'S HOUSE, I WAS behind schedule. Since I was in Savannah, I gave Kate a quick call.

"How do you feel about a trip to Miami?" I asked when she answered the phone.

"As long as it's not thirty-eight degrees like it is here, I'm on board," she said. "What's in Miami?"

"Hopefully Vince," I said. "I traced the number in his pocket to a man named Luis Vega. He's married to Angelica."

"Yikes," Kate said. "That could get sticky. Domestics make me uncomfortable. That's when people lose their minds and open fire. And we can't cross state lines armed."

"Hopefully it won't come to an all-out gun fight," I said, rolling my eyes. Kate always thought in extremes. She could really be a bummer at times. "Best-case scenario is we go, find Vince, and guilt his sorry behind back home. Worst case is that we find Angelica and get some information."

"With anyone else, I'd agree with you," Kate said.

"Are you at home or at the office?" I asked.

"I'm at home," she said. "I'll pack a bag and I can meet you if you want?"

"I'm headed your direction," I said. "I've got to stop by Mom's to look at a couple of things, and then I'll swing by after and pick you up."

I looked at the clock, knowing we'd be on a tight schedule if we were going to find Vince tonight. It was only an hour and a half flight from Savannah to Miami, and there were several flights to and from. It wouldn't leave too much time to find the hotel and get settled before heading to find Angelica.

"Expect me around noon," I said, calculating the time.

"10-4," she said and hung up.

I'd just turned onto the highway when my phone started ringing again and Rosemarie's picture popped up on the screen.

"Hello?" I said.

"Addison," Rosemarie said, a slight tinge of panic in her voice. "Scarlet ran away."

"What?" I asked. "What happened?"

"We had a difference of opinion on style, and she called me a country bumpkin bore and a bunch of other names that aren't worth repeating." Rose-marie dropped her voice down to a whisper. "I think she was just out of sorts because she missed her morning nap, and the jackhammers were giving her a migraine."

"Jackhammers?" I asked.

"After the jackhammers started she mumbled something about how she doesn't do favors for people, and then she stole the keys to your Audi and took off. I have no idea where she went. I'm so sorry I failed you. I didn't think she'd be so hard to handle, and if you let your attention slip just for a second she's off getting into stuff. She reminds me of Johnny Castle when he was a puppy."

"It's not your fault," I said, wanting desperately to ask about the jackhammers. "I put a tracker on her phone back when she was dating Ugly Mo in case she got kidnapped, so I'll find her. Umm...how long do you think this home improvement project is going to take?"

"I don't know," Rosemarie said. "Could be days. Could be weeks. Need to talk to my contractor and I'll get back with you."

"Uhh," I said, but she'd already hung up. My grip tightened on the steering wheel. "Don't think about it. Just don't think about it. The house isn't torn apart. The baby will have a lovely room to come home to, and all of those people and Rosemarie and Scarlet will be out of our house and far away."

By the time I'd finished my pep talk, I was even more uptight and anxious than I was before I started, and my deep breathing exercises were close to hyperventilation. I saw the exit for

Whiskey Bayou and veered off the highway and toward the one thing that could make everything better.

In my opinion, the people who owned the Dairy Queen in Whiskey Bayou were geniuses. It was a husband and wife couple—George and Toy Floyd—and no one knew anything about them. They were an enigma, and they'd bought the old Briar house on Marsh Road after the family lost the house to foreclosure.

There was one road in and one road out of Whiskey Bayou since the whole town backed up to the marsh, and they'd built the Dairy Queen just outside of the city limits, before the *Welcome to Whiskey Bayou* sign, so it was the first and last thing you saw as you entered or left the town. They'd gotten a good deal of my money and everyone else's over the years.

I ordered a hot fudge sundae with extra whipped cream and nuts for myself, and I ordered a hamburger and fries for the baby. The sun was shining and people were taking advantage of it even though it was still too cold to function, in my opinion.

The van was recognizable to everyone, and considering the last time they saw me barreling through town was when Savage had gotten shot, I could understand the stares and hesitant waves.

I'd finished the sundae and the fries by the time I reached the house, and I blew out a sigh of relief as I saw my Audi parked in the driveway next to the

General Lee—or at least halfway in the driveway. She got points for trying I guess.

I pulled under the giant mossy oak next to the driveway, and I decided to leave the burger in the car for a snack later. I didn't bother to lock the van. I went in the side gate to the back of the house. There was a shed and a garage behind the house, and I could see the new gazebo and pond that had been put in on the side yard. A wooden fence surrounded the back and side of the property to divide between the neighbors' yards.

I saw Edna peeping over the fence near the garage, and I remembered what Scarlet said about talking to the neighbors for information. I cut across the yard and headed toward her. She must've been standing on a box or something else, because Edna wasn't much taller than Scarlet and she was almost as old.

"Hey, Edna," I said, giving her a little wave. Edna Mohlner had been old when I'd been a kid. I never remember her having a husband, but I do remember her elderly mother had lived with her before she passed.

Edna pinched her lips and looked down at the ground, probably trying to decide if she had time to make a run for it. But she was old and I walked fast, and manners were manners.

"Addison," she said, nodding. "I went to your wedding. It was real nice of you to invite everyone like that. But I guess now that you're rich you can afford to do things like that."

"My husband is rich," I said, smiling. "I'm still just me."

"Of course, it would've been nicer had that poor FBI agent not gotten shot," she said. "It seems like bad people just follow you around. My grandmother always used to say that you're known by the company you keep."

I smiled again and put my hand up to my forehead to block the sun as I looked up at her. "Do you know Vince Walker?" I asked. "He and Mom got married last year. I'm sure you've seen him around the yard."

"I know Vince," she said. "He's a Walker. And Walkers built this town. That's his family's distillery Scarlet Holmes gave you." Edna pressed her lips together. "I remember Scarlet when I was a girl, and it's a miracle there's any man left in town to call property his own."

I couldn't really dispute the truth. Scarlet had always said God wouldn't have made her beautiful and savvy if he hadn't wanted her to take over the world.

"When was the last time you saw Vince?" I asked.

"About three days ago," she said. "Before the crack of dawn. Looked like he was loading his truck down for a trip."

"Did he say anything to you?" I asked.

"He told me good morning. He always does." She pursed her lips as she thought. "Then he said he was taking a fishing trip for a few days, and to keep an eye on things here for him. That's ridiculous, of course, I can't spend twenty-four hours a day watching over the neighborhood."

I thanked her and wished her a good day, and then I walked toward the shed. The garage was my mother's domain. When I was a kid, that's where she'd done her Jane Fonda workouts and watched TV if my dad was home and had the house TV occupied. The shed and the garage were strictly adult zones, though Phoebe and I had tried to look in the windows from time to time. Entrance was forbidden, which made us want to see inside all the more.

When I was sixteen I'd gotten my shot. The door had been left unlocked by some miracle and Bobby Wallace and I had snuck in to have a major make-out session. Since Bobby Wallace had been the quarterback of the football team, the captain of the swim team, and there was a rumor going around that the bulge in his Speedo was all natural, it seemed like the chance of a lifetime.

What I didn't know, and would have if I'd understood context clues, was that the door was unlocked for a reason. Bobby was barely past first base when the door slammed open and a gaggle of cackling women barged in. My mom played bridge on Sunday nights, and she and the ladies had decided to make a trip for ice cream in between games.

I'd been so hot for Bobby I hadn't noticed the wine glasses or the table set up with cards. Unfortunately for Bobby, his mother got an eyeful and he got shipped off to military school for the rest of his senior year. No one had seen him since.

That experience had cured me of ever wanting to see in my parents' private sanctums, and I never tested my luck again.

When I reached my dad's shed, I was relieved to find the door locked. The way my mother had talked, it sounded like we'd be ready for war at a moment's notice. I trudged back to the house and my mother opened the door before I got there.

"What did Edna have to say?" she asked, looking both ways before quickly shutting the door behind me. "She knows something is up. She's been looking over her fence all morning."

"She said she hasn't seen Vince in three days, and he told her he was going fishing."

My mother snorted. "I'm telling you, that man has never fished a day in his life. Hunting and fishing are his least favorite things to do on the planet. He said he hunted humans for most of his life, so he has no desire to do it to animals."

"I guess I can see his point," I said. "But I needed a timeline and Edna gave it to me. You didn't hear him leave? He didn't leave a note?"

She crossed her arms and gnawed at her thumbnail. "I was mad, and I told him I was tired of being ignored, and then I went out and slept in the garage. I didn't hear him leave. He sent me a text saying he loved me and he'd call when he could, but that was three days ago and I haven't heard from him since. What if he didn't leave? What if something happened to him?"

I was glad to know she'd worked through her anger to see there were other possibilities.

"I need to get into Dad's shed," I said. "Do you know where the key is?"

It was so ingrained to deny entrance that she hesitated before nodding and going to rummage around in a kitchen drawer. "I put it in the junk drawer," she said. "Do you need something to eat? You look a little peaky."

"I've got a burger," I said. "Is Scarlet here? I saw my car out front."

"Ssh," my mother said, putting her hand over my mouth, her eyes wide with panic. "You'll wake her up."

"What's she doing here?" I asked.

"She said this was the only place she could get peace and quiet for her morning nap. I asked her why she didn't just go to a hotel, but she was kind of closed-lipped about the whole thing."

"She got banned," I said.

"Huh, maybe I'll try that." Mom blew out a breath. "At least she's sleeping for now. No one makes me pop Xanax like that woman does."

"I didn't know you popped Xanax," I said.

"I don't do it often anymore," she said. "Sometimes I'll take them before I get a massage because it makes me tense when they rub me. And I always take one when I go Black Friday shopping because I've found they enhance my reflexes."

"I don't think that's how they're supposed to work," I said.

"I dunno," she said, shrugging. "But I took two as soon as Scarlet got here and the urge to strangle her in her sleep has disappeared. I'm going to make you some cookies to take with you. I want to make sure you give birth to one of those cute chubby babies. Gladys Pike's granddaughter came out looking like a scarecrow. Scared me to death. Gladys still isn't speaking to me because I screamed. But I don't care what anybody says, there are such things as ugly babies."

I smiled tightly and crept out the back door so as not to wake Scarlet, and I made my way back across the yard to the shed. Edna had moved to her porch swing and was bundled up like an Eskimo, but she was still watching the house with a great deal of interest. Probably waiting for Scarlet to come out.

My dad had replaced the shed door with a solid, regular-size exterior door. There were no windows. It was just a plain shed the size of a small bedroom with panel siding and a tin roof. I stuck the key in the doorknob and turned. It opened smoothly, and I pushed it open wide, more nervous than I'd expected to be.

It was just a room. Just a space. No different than any other. It was always difficult to lose a parent, no matter what your relationship. And to lose a father who was barely in his fifties and had seemed so alive before his death was even more difficult. I didn't dwell on him being gone, but being slapped in the face with the memories was another thing entirely.

I reached inside and felt for a light switch and flicked them on. The fluorescent lights flickered and hummed before coming on bright white. I blinked a couple of times and then stepped into the room, leaving the door open.

It was a simple room, with brown wood panel walls and two brown leather recliners and a small sofa crammed at one end. There was a TV and three rows of file cabinets. On the remaining bit of wall was a built-in shelf with guns and enough ammunition to hold down the fort during a zombie apocalypse.

I immediately went to the file cabinets, noticing the dust had been disturbed there. I opened them one by one, not sure what I was looking for and not even sure if I'd recognize it if I found it.

"You're doing it all wrong," Scarlet said from behind me.

I jumped a foot and grabbed my chest as my heart stopped. "You scared me to death," I said.

She smiled. "I'm good at that."

"I thought you were napping," I said.

"I was just faking," she said. "I got ears like a bat, and your mother whispers like a freight train. I climbed out the window when I heard you come back here. I would've gotten here before you started muttering under your breath, but my coat got stuck in the window. Then when I pulled it free I fell in the bushes."

I looked her over carefully and noticed the twigs in her hair and her coat was starting to look like a taxidermied muskrat with mange. The last time I'd seen her she was wearing her morning turban, but she'd decided on a jet-black bob for today's hair. I hated to say it, but she looked deranged.

"What am I doing wrong?" I asked. The faster I moved this along, the faster Kate and I could head to Miami.

"Tricks of the trade," Scarlet said. "You're looking for the last file that Vince read, right?"

"Right," I said.

"Look at the dust trail," she said. "Vince started in the same place you are right now. If he'd found anything there the trail would've stopped."

"Oh," I said, understanding what she was saying. The disturbance in the dust stopped on the last file cabinet at the top drawer. I opened it carefully.

The drawer was full of manila folders, all stuffed with papers and reports. Everything was written in my dad's neat block lettering.

"Great," I said. "I don't have time to go through all of these."

"Stand aside, girl," Scarlet said. "People are always the same, even the trained ones. Human habits are hard to break."

I raised a brow. I had no idea what she was talking about, but I squished as far as I could into the corner so there was room for Scarlet and her coat.

But I watched as Scarlet ran her fingers over the top of the files, as if she were searching for what she was looking for by touch instead of with her eyes.

"There it is," she said, and pulled on the file, trying to get it out, but it was squeezed in tight. I moved in to help her, and I yanked hard until it came free. The cabinet rattled and I was left holding a heavy file in my hands.

"How do you know that this is the one?" I asked.

"Because your father, may he rest in peace, was a creature of habit," she said. "I've never met a more anal son of a gun in my life. You forget I knew him since he was a boy, and I loved him like he was family, but Charlie would bore you to tears. He was no fun at all." She rapped her chest with her fist twice and then kissed her fingers like an Italian mob boss. "Bless his soul." As if that made up for calling a dead man an anal son of a gun.

"Every file in there is perfectly ordered and alphabetized," she said. "The folders are the same size and brand, the handwriting is the same, and the way your father placed papers inside the folders is the same. All except for this one. It was sticking up, as if Vince hadn't quite been able to get it all the way back in, and the papers are just kind of stuck in there."

"Wow," I said. I could honestly say that was the

first time since Scarlet had been accompanying me during my investigations that she'd actually helped.

"And for a little bonus tip," she said, "Always feel around at the bottom for things that might fall." She slipped her tiny wrinkled hand into the empty space where the file had been, and I heard the rattle again.

"What is that?" I asked, leaning over the drawer to see inside since I was about eight inches taller than Scarlet.

"It's a key," she said. "And I know what it goes to." She pulled out a tiny silver key, like one you'd use for a gym locker.

"How do you know what it goes to?" I asked.

"Because I was snooping around in your father's office while your mother thought I was sleeping," she said, conspiratorially. "Pretty sneaky, huh?"

"Pretty sneaky," I said, nodding in agreement. "So what does it go to?"

"I'll show you mine, if you show me yours," she said. "What are you planning, Addison Holmes?"

I blew out a breath, knowing unequivocally that all the plans I'd made in my head were about to change. "I found the woman Vince was communicating with in Miami. Kate and I are headed down there this afternoon."

Scarlet nodded, as if she knew what I was going to say. "I've already got my bag packed. I wouldn't mind a trip to Miami."

CHAPTER NINE

I LEFT MY MOTHER'S HOUSE WITH A BAG OF cookies and Aunt Scarlet, so things weren't quite as bad as they could've been. I figured I could go over the file on the plane. I didn't care what was in it, so long as it led to Vince and this whole thing could be put behind us. I was starting to get an icky feeling in my gut that had nothing to do with morning sickness.

When I pulled up to Kate's right at noon, she was out the door and as punctual as ever. She had her matching and sturdy carry-on and computer bag, and she was wearing a pair of jeans with the cuffs rolled, white sneakers, and a light sweater the color of marigolds. That was Kate's idea of Miami chic.

Kate lived in the "historic" part of Whiskey Bayou, where the houses were a century old and there was land between neighbors. Where the mossy oaks provided shade and were sturdy enough to hang swings from the branches.

Kate opened the side door of the van to toss her luggage in, and came face to face with Scarlet. She froze and then looked at me. I gave her a thin smile and shrugged.

"Hi, Scarlet," Kate said. "I wasn't expecting to see you."

"I like to keep people on their toes," she said. "And I never pass up a trip to Miami. As long as we stay a hundred feet or more away from the Copacabana Lounge, I'm in good shape."

"It's always good to know your boundaries," Kate said without batting an eye. "Do you want to sit in the front?"

"No, I like it back here. If I lie on my back I can feel the vibrations from the road. Not much wakes my lady parts up nowadays."

"Well, have fun," Kate said. She shut the side door and then got in front with me.

"What time is our flight?" Kate asked.

"There's one at two thirty and another at four," I said. "I wasn't a hundred percent sure what our timeline would be like, so I figured we could buy the tickets when we got there."

"I forgot you travel like a barbarian," Kate said. "I don't do lines, and the less people I have to be around the better."

"I like an aisle seat," Scarlet said. "I don't like crawling over people when I have to go to the bathroom. Makes me feel like I'm giving lap dances, and I gave that up years ago. It's hard on the back."

"I'll get Lucy to make the arrangements," Kate said. "We've got plenty of time to make the two thirty. The sooner we get there, the sooner we can get in touch with Vince's mystery woman. And you know what that means?"

I looked at her, confused. "The sooner we can have dinner and go to bed?" I asked.

Scarlet snorted from the back seat. "That baby has made you a real dud. This is Miami, girl. And you're not a Holmes in Miami until you have a restraining order against you at a club. I've had at least one since 1976. They even got my picture up by the door at the Copacabana."

"It's Miami," Kate said. "We can eat and dance, and then eat some more. And then we can order dessert from room service at midnight. And we can watch the moon over the water from our balcony."

"I don't think we have a balcony," I said. "I just grabbed something quick and easy near the airport."

"You should probably cancel those," Kate said. "Lucy made us reservations at the Four Seasons. If you do Miami, you have to do it in style."

"I feel like I'm taking a much different trip than the two of you," I said.

I circled around the airport what felt like half a dozen times before Kate finally suggested that I go with valet parking and the agency would cover the cost just so she and Scarlet didn't have to walk a hundred miles.

"Wait a second," I said once we got out of the van and the valet attendant handed us our luggage.

The man was dressed in a valet uniform of brown pants and a matching shirt. He was moving so quickly he didn't seem to need a jacket. He paused where he was and raised his brows.

"Aunt Scarlet," I said. "You know you can't take any weapons with you."

Kate blew out a breath and set her luggage down, and then walked over to talk to the valet guys as a distraction.

"I'm an old lady," Scarlet said. "They wouldn't let an old lady travel to Miami without some protection. That's un-American."

"It's also against the law," I said. "Hand over your gun."

I held out my hand and waited, and Scarlet narrowed her eyes at me, no doubt trying to see whether or not I was bluffing.

"Fine," she said. "But I'm going to see my guy once I get to the city. I don't like being unarmed. Sometimes fights break out in the clubs, and you gotta shoot holes in stuff."

"Like people?" I asked, appalled.

"Sometimes," she said. "Sometimes the ceiling or bathroom stalls or speakers 'cause the bass is too loud. Guns are real handy. You should get one."

"I have one," I said.

"Where is it?" she asked. "You're not pulling a fast one on me, are you? I'm not leaving my gun if you have yours."

"My gun is at home where it's supposed to be," I told her patiently.

"That's fine then," she said, digging in her bag and pulling out a .44 revolver.

"Have you ever shot this thing?" I asked, unloading it and then hiding the bullet and the gun in a cabinet inside the van.

"Of course I've shot it," she said. "Kicks like a mule. Broke my face once and I got to wear an eye patch."

"What else do you have in there?" I asked. "A knife?"

"Maybe," she said. "Don't tell me ladies can't carry knives either?"

"I know you know the rules," I said. "You fly all over the world."

"Yeah, but most of the time they don't even notice I'm carrying," she said. "They let old people get away with all kinds of stuff. I saw a man in a wheelchair who was on oxygen board with a sawed-off shotgun once. I think old people make those TSA folks nervous."

"You may be right," I said. "But just for the sake of time, go ahead and take out all your weapons so we don't get detained."

Scarlet snapped her teeth together and then dumped her handbag on the floor of the van. Along with three knives in varying lengths, she had brass knuckles, a Chinese throwing star and a can of Mace.

I was curious about the brass knuckles and the

throwing star, but I closed the sliding door of the van, hefted Scarlet's bags, and then we followed Kate into the airport.

Nick and I had flown first class to Tahiti, and I'd quickly become accustomed to no-hassle travel.

"I've got lots of tricks to get you through the airport quick," Scarlet said. "Y'all stick with me and we'll be on that flight in no time. People are real scared of old ladies. Especially if you pretend like you're about to die."

"That would certainly scare me," Kate said.

Thankfully, the airport wasn't crowded. Scarlet stood in front of us and charged her way through oncoming crowds, sticking out a foot from time to time and throwing the occasional elbow. When a policeman came up, I was sure he'd seen her clothesline a woman more interested in her phone than her surroundings, but he offered to help get her through security and to our gate as quickly as possible.

By the time we got to our seats, I was out of breath and regretting packing so many pairs of shoes in my carry-on. Kate and I were seated together in the front row, and Scarlet was across the aisle from us, sizing up her seatmate. He was a nice-looking man in his sixties in Wranglers and a sport coat, and he stowed his Stetson in the overhead compartment, showing a thick mane of silver hair.

"Oh, Lord," I said, nudging Kate.

She snickered. "That's what you get for bringing her along."

"It wasn't my fault," I said. "She blackmailed me."

"Play stupid games, win stupid prizes."

"I'm going to need a gin and tonic for me and my new friend here," Scarlet said to the flight attendant. "And you're going to want to keep them coming on account of I look a lot better after I'm blurry."

The flight attendant nodded automatically, but I could tell by the look in her eyes there was a part of her brain that was blaring a warning signal. But she went off to start passing out drinks, and I figured at that point she had no one to blame but herself.

"So what's going on with Vince?" Kate asked, once we'd taken off. "Find out anything new?"

I'd been reading the file I'd found in my dad's shed while we'd been waiting for takeoff. "I'm not sure," I said. "And I'm not sure what any of this has to do with Vince missing, or if it's even related." I showed her the key we found at the bottom of the file cabinet drawer.

"What's this?" she asked.

"Scarlet was snooping in my dad's office and said she'd looked through the trash and the desk. She found the address for one of the storage lockers in Whiskey Bayou. I called and talked to the manager, and he said my dad has had an account with them for years. He said he paid outright for the space."

"And this key opens the storage space?" Kate asked.

"I don't know, but I'm going to try it when we get back home."

"What's the case file?"

"That's the weird thing," I said. "I don't think this was an official case file. It's my dad's notes, but it's not written like his other formal reports. Almost as if he were keeping track and making notes to himself."

"That's not unusual," Kate said.

"Do you remember the de Salva case?" I asked. "We were kids when it went down. I don't remember much. Just that Dad was gone more than usual, and there were a couple of times when cops did drive-bys to make sure we were okay."

"I remember," Kate said. "And then when I went through the police academy we studied the case. It was a joint task force operation with the FBI, DEA, and Savannah police department, and it was a RICO case involving Carmen de Salva and his whole operation."

"Who's Rico?" I asked.

"No, RICO," she said. "Racketeer Influenced and Corrupt Organizations."

"Oh," I said. "So Dad and Vince were working this case with the Feds?"

"Them and a couple of other guys," Kate said. "It was a huge case. Carmen de Salva had a monopoly on most of southern Georgia. Construction companies, garbage services, the dry-cleaning industry—you name it—de Salva owned it. But that's what made it difficult to track. He owned

what looked like on paper were competing businesses, so if Bob's construction company and Joe's
construction company competed for the same huge
contracts, one of them would bid at an exorbitant
price range, and the other would bid even higher,
making the exorbitant price not look so bad after
all. You're talking millions and millions of dollars
the city was paying to Carmen de Salva."

"How'd he get caught?" I asked.

"When drugs and bodies started littering the
streets," Kate said. "De Salva owned Savannah and
all of the surrounding small cities and islands. They
were bringing cocaine in, and then using some of
the dummy corporations as a holding zone. And
then the DA was killed execution style, and his wife
and kids were found in their car inside their garage.
They died of carbon monoxide poising. Except the
locks to the car had been melted shut and their
hands had been tied.

"The task federal task force was put together
after the DA was killed, and the Feds kept your dad
and Vince on the team since they'd done so much of
the legwork. The de Salva organization went far and
wide, and the task force started applying pressure to
de Salva by targeting the higher-ups in his organization, most of whom were family members.

"They arrested two of his sons-in-law, his
nephew, his son, his brother-in-law, and his uncle
and charged them with every little thing they could
throw at them. Of course, that pissed de Salva off
and he started doubling down. The FBI special

agent in charge died in a freak car accident. A DEA agent had his throat slit in a gas station parking lot in broad daylight. No one saw a thing. It's no wonder your place had extra protection at night. De Salva was gunning for everyone involved."

"Wow," I said. "I don't know how my mother did it, but she deserves a medal, because Phoebe and I had no clue we were in any kind of danger."

"I didn't know most of it until I was in the academy," she said. "The only problem with the whole thing was de Salva maintained his innocence through it all. He swore over and over again that he never had anything to do with drugs. According to de Salva, someone else was using the situation to move the drugs in, and whoever it was killed the agents involved with the case. He even agreed to plead guilty to the racketeering charges in exchange for dropping the drug and murder charges."

"I'm guessing they didn't fall for that," I said.

"No, they went for the whole shebang, and they sent de Salva to prison, along with everyone else they could scoop up with him."

"Did de Salva say who was responsible for bringing the drugs in?" I asked.

"I don't know," she said, shrugging. "But I did read that de Salva had died in prison a couple of months back."

"Huh," I said, raising my brows. "That's an interesting development." I looked over at Scarlet, and she and her new cowboy friend were both fast asleep, and Scarlet's head was resting on his shoulder.

"Do you think if we just left her there they'd take her back to Savannah?" Kate asked in a whisper.

"No, but maybe we can borrow one of the wheelchairs and push her to a cab."

"She's going to love that," Kate said, sarcastically. Everyone knew Scarlet was anti-wheelchair or anything else that made her seem old.

"Look on the bright side," I said. "Her gun and her brass knuckles are back in the van."

CHAPTER TEN

"Oh, thank you, Lord," I said as we got out of the cab at the entry of the Four Seasons.

I rested my hands on my knees and bent over, taking deep breaths. The cab had smelled like old tacos and Axe, and I'd stuck my head out like a dog most of the way to keep my stomach under control.

"There's sunshine and it's eighty degrees," Kate said, "I might have to move here until Savannah has decided it's done with winter."

"It's always summer in Miami," Scarlet said. "And when it's not, there's a hurricane. I brought my special thong so I could catch some rays. Miami isn't prudish like the cruise ship. I love Miami. They don't care how old your moneymaker is so long as you shake it."

"I saw y'all's pictures from the nudist colony," Kate whispered. "I had nightmares for weeks. I'm not sure I can do a topless beach with Scarlet."

"The key is to always look just above her head,"

I said. "She's got a lot of things below the neck you don't want to make eye contact with. Let's go drop the bags in the room and let me change into something more Miami, and then I want to get a look at Luis and Angelica Vega's house before it gets dark. Once we get the lay of the land, we can figure out how to approach her tomorrow."

Lucy had reserved us a connecting suite, so Kate and I took the side with two queen beds and we let Scarlet have the other side to herself so everyone could get a good night's sleep. I washed my face, and decided on a bright yellow jumpsuit that exposed my shoulders and showed off my new cleavage to its best advantage. It was fortunate I'd spent the last few weeks in Tahiti and gotten a tan, otherwise my pasty winter color would've clashed. I added a thin black belt and black wedge half boots, and then I dabbed on extra concealer because I was looking a little gaunt.

Twenty minutes later, Scarlet was asleep in her connecting suite and I was waiting for Kate to come out of the bathroom. She never took this long to change clothes and I was starting to worry something might be wrong when the lock clicked and Kate came out.

My mouth dropped open. Kate was a creature of habit. She liked plain colors and plain clothes and didn't like to draw attention to herself. Everyone always underestimated Kate. Which apparently made her good at her job. People told her all kinds of ridiculous things because she looked harmless.

"Wha—wha—who?" I stuttered.

"I've never actually seen you speechless before."

I opened my mouth to say something, but she was right. I was speechless.

"Now you can't hound me for never wearing lipstick," she said, puckering her bright red lips.

"Where did you get leather pants?" I asked.

"The kids' section at Nordstrom," she said. "It's weird what people let their children wear. And don't even ask how I got them on. You might have to rub my legs to get the blood circulating again once I take them off."

"Good call on the backless shirt," I said, admiring the bright red. It draped all the way to her lower back, showing the little dimple on each side of her spine.

"Well, you got all the boobs, so I figured I should work with what I've got instead of trying to compete."

"I feel like I'm having an out-of-body experience," I said. "I caught my roommate in college smoking a joint once, and I accidentally inhaled. Maybe I've lost too many brain cells."

"Sometimes the job calls for blending in," she said. "I would've stuck out like a sore thumb in my other clothes. When in Rome, right?" She put a hand on her hip and turned from side to side in front of the mirror.

I figured beggars couldn't be choosers, so I didn't say anything when she put on a pair of plain black ballet flats instead of the stilettos I would've chosen. Kate liked for her feet to be flat on the ground for some weird reason. She wore flats to our prom and sneakers to her wedding.

We walked down to the lobby and waited while the concierge brought us the keys for one of the resort Mercedes to use at our leisure.

"What's that squeaking sound?" I asked.

"My thighs," Kate said. "Maybe I should've used more Vaseline."

The concierge gave me the keys and a last lingering look at Kate's butt, and we were directed to a sweet little two-door roadster.

"This seems like a bad idea," I told Kate. "What kind of place would just give people the keys to expensive cars and expect to get them back in one piece?"

"Expensive places," Kate said. "Give me the keys."

"No way," I said.

"You're a terrible driver."

"No, I'm not," I said. "You're just a control freak. All cops are."

"Maybe if you learned to use turn signals and read the speed limit signs I'd let you drive," she said, getting behind the wheel.

"I think your pants are so tight they're squeezing your brain," I said. "Driving should be an experience. Besides, I'm an excellent driver. My dad would sneak me out on the training course and let me drive his squad car through maneuvers before I had my license. You're just a stick-in-the-mud."

Kate pouted while I typed Angelica Vega's address into the GPS.

"She lives in the Upper East Side," I said.

"I'm hoping that's a good part of town," Kate said.

"It's on the bay," I said. "We're going straight up the coast."

By the time we were halfway there I remembered why Kate and I usually took separate cars when we had to go to the same place.

"GPS said this was a fifteen-minute drive," I said. "We're going on twenty-five. Maybe you could press your foot down on that thing we like to call the accelerator, grandma. You can't wear pants like that and not speed. It's the law."

"I'm pretty sure the law in Miami is just like the law in the rest of the country," Kate said. "I'm getting us there safe. *All* of us."

"He's well protected. I could give birth before we get there," I complained.

"He?" Kate asked. "There's no way you're having a boy. You look like hell. Only girls do that to their mothers."

"That's an old wives' tale," I said, flipping down the visor mirror. "I don't even know why I bother putting on makeup. I look like Natalie Portman in that movie where she was a dancer and could only eat an apple and smoke a cigarette a day."

"You look fine," Kate said. "Nobody is going to be paying us any attention anyway. Everyone here is gorgeous. Do all these people spend every waking minute at the gym? I haven't seen a man yet without a six-pack."

"I just need more concealer," I said, ignoring Kate and digging in my bag. "And mascara. Concealer and mascara are gifts from the Lord."

"Tammy Faye Bakker always thought so," Kate said. "I still don't think we're going to find Vince. This is completely out of character."

"I can fill up notebooks with the men through history who have done things out of character because of sex," I said.

By the time Kate turned onto Bay Street, I was wishing I'd put deodorant in my bag. Nerves were getting the best of me. I'd spent the entire trip blocking the thought that I very well might run into Vince while I was here. Even worse was the thought of what I might be interrupting when I found him. There was also the reality that he might not want to come home at all.

I could no longer pretend this wasn't actually happening, and my body recognized the added stress by making sure I was sweating like Meghan Markle at a royal family reunion. Whoever this Angelica woman was, she knew Vince, and Vince was who I needed to find. And then it was up to my mother to decide whether or not he lived.

Kate drove down the street and around the block and then did another pass-by.

"There it is," she said, pointing to a cute little two-story cottage in white stucco. It had bright red shutters and a red arched door, and a black iron railing balcony on the second floor. The front yard was miniscule, and most of it was covered with palm trees and luscious tropical flowers. The front of the house faced the bay.

Kate kept driving and pulled into a small parking lot where people could get access to the beach. The lot was empty and so was the beach below us.

"This neighborhood is weird," I told Kate. "Where are all the people?"

"I don't know," she said. "It is kind of weird though. I guess it's not too late for them to still be at work. I only see one car parked in a driveway, and there's a car parked on the street on the other side of the block."

I looked up at the sky. It was a gorgeous, bright day, and the sun was setting across the water.

"It's creepy if you ask me," I said. "I don't know what Vince was thinking."

"So what's the plan?" Kate asked.

"I don't know," I said. "I thought you might have a plan."

"Why would I have a plan? I came to Miami to walk on the beach and drink martinis. I'm just along for the ride."

"If you were just along for the ride then you shouldn't have driven," I said triumphantly.

Kate blew out a breath. "When was the last time you or your mother called Vince?"

"Mom told me his phone is going directly to voicemail," I said. And then I felt like a dummy because I hadn't bothered to try Vince's phone. That was PI 101—always check the most obvious first.

I found Vince's number in my contacts, and then I waited for it to ring.

"Straight to voicemail," I said, confirming.

"I can probably get Savage to trace his last known location if we come up with a dead end here," Kate said. "Your mom might have to come to terms that filing a missing persons report is the best way to get him back. Especially if he's been digging around in that old RICO case. He might be in more trouble than he bargained for."

"I don't suppose you have any binoculars," I asked, squinting at the front of Angelica's house.

"Of course I do." Kate dug around in her giant designer bag and came up with camouflaged travel-sized binoculars.

"Cute," I said. "You should get some in pink camo. I've got a pair of pants that would match."

"Yes, because that would make you completely unnoticeable."

"It would in Miami," I said.

I looked through the binoculars and scanned along the street line. We'd passed a marker on the way into the Upper East Side that proclaimed the area as the historic district, and all of the houses looked similar to Angelica's.

"I can't see anything," I said. "The driveway is on the other side, but I don't remember seeing a car in the driveway. Maybe you should go check it out. See if anything looks hinky."

"Sure, Velma," Kate said. "Let me get right on that."

"Here," I said, digging in my purse. "Take my big sunglasses and a scarf to tie over your head. That'll be cute, it matches your shirt. If someone stops you just say we had car trouble or something and you were walking to get help."

"And tell me again why you aren't going?"

"I can't walk in these shoes," I said. "That's what you get for advocating for comfort."

"Whatever," she said, resigned. "Why don't I just say I'm taking a walk along the beach?"

I pointed to the sign I'd just noticed while I'd been lecturing Kate. "It's a private beach for residents only," I said. "Besides, no one walks on the beach in leather pants. Do you know what would happen to your thighs if you mixed sand and Vaseline?"

Kate squenched her nose. "Fine," she said. "I'll walk the block. Maybe I'll see Vince's car parked somewhere."

"Leave your phone in here," I told her. "If you need an excuse you can always knock on a door and ask to use the phone. It'll look suspicious if you have your phone with you."

"Come get behind the driver's seat and leave the car running just in case anything goes wrong," she said.

I got out of the car and hurried to the other side

to wait for Kate to get out. "I miss the old days of surveillance. We should've stopped at that taco stand before we left the city. The baby could use a snack."

"I've got trail mix in my bag," Kate said, squeaking her way across the parking lot.

I got into the driver's side of the car and adjusted the seat, making myself comfortable. I dug through Kate's bag until I found the trail mix. She also had potato chips, a crossword puzzle, a scrunchie, and a small caliber pistol. I raised my brows at that, wondering when she'd gotten a gun and how she'd snuck it in there without me knowing about it.

Kate had disappeared down the end of the street, so I passed the time by pressing all of the high-tech buttons in the Mercedes and flipping through the radio stations. I'd finished the trail mix and was working my way through a pack of gum when I thought I saw movement down the street. I grabbed the binoculars and searched around Angelica's house, my attention caught by a small dog in a red sweater roaming the front yard. It hadn't been there before.

The car door opened and Kate slid in beside me, but I kept my eyes on the dog, thinking surely its owner wouldn't be far behind.

"Do you see that dog?" I asked. "Isn't it cute? It's so tiny. Maybe Nick and I could get a dog."

"It's my neighbor's," a voice said. It was Hispanic with a heavy accent—definitely not Kate's.

I jerked my head and whacked myself in the eye with the binoculars. I'd never seen the woman sitting next to me. She was petite in stature and probably in her late fifties or early sixties, but her skin was smooth and much younger looking. It was always the eyes that gave age away. Her dark hair was slicked back from her face, her lashes were long enough for their own zip code, and her lips were pouty and slicked crimson.

Despite her beauty, there was a coldness to her, and she didn't look like she was interested in a neighborly chat. Especially with the gun sitting casually in her lap and her hand wrapped around it.

CHAPTER ELEVEN

"WELL, HELLO THERE," I SAID, MY EYES FIXED ON the gun. She didn't seem to be in too much of hurry to point it directly at me, so I took the chance and met her gaze. I was still holding on to the binoculars, so I rested my hands on the steering wheel so she didn't get too jumpy.

"I don't mean to be rude," I said, after we stared at each other in silence a couple of minutes, "but I usually like to know the person who's holding a gun on me. My purse is right there between your feet. Just take whatever you want."

"I don't want your money," she said, insulted. "Start driving."

I knew this was a bad idea. Driving to an undisclosed location where she could shoot me and it would take people days to find my body seemed worse than being shot in a parking lot where Kate could at least find me easily.

She must have seen my hesitation because she

picked up the gun and put it too close to my temple for my peace of mind. I swallowed hard, and I felt a part of my brain tuck itself away like a turtle in a shell—a protective measure to keep me from screaming my head off and getting shot in the face. I'd been held at gunpoint before. I wished I could say it got easier every time, but it didn't.

"I'm going to put down the binoculars nice and slow. And then I'll drive wherever you want to go. Okay?"

"Just do it," she said, waving the gun impatiently.

I felt a little bit of relief that her finger wasn't on the trigger. At least she knew what she was doing with a weapon. As ridiculous as it sounded, I would much rather have someone with experience holding a gun on me than some moron with a happy trigger finger.

I put the binoculars down and then grasped the wheel. I was having déjà vu. If I got through this alive, I vowed to make this a learning experience just like when I'd been held at gunpoint in my van on my wedding day. I'd learned to always check the back seat for psychopaths, and now I'd learned to always lock the car doors when sitting alone in a parking lot.

This is what happened when you grew up in a small town with a nonexistent crime rate. You always thought the best of people, and then *BAM*, you got hijacked out of the blue.

"Hello?" the lady asked, waving the gun again.

"I'm threatening you. Are you a crazy woman or something?"

I almost started laughing hysterically. I couldn't figure out how to put the car in drive, and when I didn't look at her face she sounded exactly like Rosie Perez.

"I don't know how to drive this car," I said, my voice pitching higher as I accidentally turned on the wipers. My face flushed hot and I could feel the tears threatening to fall. I was a powder keg of hormones and irrational thoughts. One of us was probably going to die, and I was really hoping it would be her.

"Good grief," she said, putting the gun down enough to reach over and click what looked like the blinker. "You never drove a Mercedes before?" Then she pursed her lips together and said, "Trash."

I was too relieved to be moving forward to be offended by her calling me trash. I snuck a quick look at the woman, and felt myself relax a little. It was hard to get too worked up when Rosie Perez was your kidnapper. She was the epitome of Miami. She had a small curvy body wrapped in turquoise spandex, big chunky jewelry, and earrings that touched her shoulders. She was the kind of woman who oozed sex appeal and for whom age was just a number. I envied that confidence.

I looked frantically for Kate as I crept slowly through the neighborhood, and I still hadn't seen a sign that humans existed in this part of town. What kind of ridiculously private place was this that no one was watching me be abducted from their kitchen window? This would've never happened in Whiskey Bayou.

I could only assume that Kate was on her way around the block, so I went the opposite direction in the hopes we'd collide as she circled back.

When we passed the corner house the woman rolled down her window and went off into a tirade of hand motions and Spanish, none of which my high school Spanish had prepared me for. She ended it by giving the sign of the cross and spitting toward her neighbor's house.

"Diablo!" she shouted.

That I understood. "Who *are* you?" I asked.

"I gotta better question for you," she said, pointing a scarlet nail in my direction. "What are you and that tiny girl doing in my neighborhood? You think I can't spot a surveillance team? I'm Puerto Rican. I can spot cops and con men a mile away. Which one are you?"

"Wait a second," I said. "You're Angelica. Angelica Vega?"

"Who wants to know?" she asked.

"The picture in your file looks nothing like you."

"I should hope not," she said. "Now, I'm only going to ask one more time. Why are you here? Who sent you?"

It seemed like a bad time to point out that was two questions, and I was about to reach the point where I could no longer drive six miles an hour while I waited for Kate to show up.

"I think there's been a misunderstanding," I said. "I'm just looking for Vince Walker. Is he here?"

"You know Vinny?" she asked, black eyes bright with curiosity.

"I'm his stepdaughter," I explained. "He went missing and my mother is freaking out."

Angelica started laughing, and the hair stood up on the back of my neck. Only crazy people laughed when they were kidnapping someone.

"He's missing and your mother thought he ran away with me," she said, wiping her eyes. "I am flattered."

"I'll make sure to tell her," I said. "Maybe you could stop waving the gun. I'm pregnant and my hormones aren't as stable as they used to be. I might start crying or I might become a screaming banshee. There's really no in-between right now."

"Ah, yes. I remember," she said, waving her hands some more. She was a very animated woman. She put the gun back in her lap. "There, is that better? Don't try anything funny because I'm fast and I'll shoot."

"I'm pregnant!"

"Pssh," she said. "So you say. Oldest trick in the book. Now please stop talking and let me think. You're giving me a headache. This is the reason I told Vince to let sleeping dogs lie. If someone like you can track me down, then anyone can."

"Hey, I happen to be a private investigator," I said. "I've got skills."

"This is Miami," she said. "They would eat your

skinny white ass for lunch and toss you into the bay."

It was at that moment I saw Kate, standing on the corner at the stop sign. She had the look on her face she gets when she's cursing in her head.

"Are those doll clothes?" Angelica asked. "I've never seen leather pants that tiny. She's built like a small boy."

I sighed. "She got them at the children's section at Nordstrom. She'll call the police if I don't let her know I'm okay."

I hoped Angelica didn't realize that was Kate's phone sitting on the console.

Angelica let out a fresh outburst of Spanish again and then said in English, "You are already more trouble than I want to deal with. In the old days, you'd have been someone's mistress. And when they got tired of you, *BOOM! BOOM!*"

She said it so loud I jerked back in my seat. "Boom boom?" I asked.

"Double tap to the brain," she said. "That's what mistresses who cause trouble get. Big mess."

"I'm married," I said, not sure now was the best time to ask what the heck she was talking about.

"Hush, Double Tap," she said, pinching my mouth closed with her fingers. "That's what I'm going to call you from now on. Double Tap."

I'd never had a nickname before, and it's not one I would've chosen for myself, but I'd always been told if you chose your own nickname that it lacked significance.

I squeaked, completely out of my element, and I looked at Kate in panic.

"Why you making noises, Double Tap?" she asked. "Pull over and tell your friend to get in the car. I want to keep moving in case you brought anyone else to my doorstep."

I was almost positive this was the exact opposite of what Nick had in mind when he told me to be careful and have a good time. I pulled over and rolled down the passenger side window, but Kate didn't move, and I couldn't read what she was thinking. Kate had a heck of a poker face.

"This is Angelica," I told Kate. "You can get in the back seat. She probably won't kill us."

"I'm undecided," Angelica said, looking Kate over. "What are you? Fourteen? You need breasts. You can buy them like mine. And even short legs like yours would look okay in these heels." She took off her shoe and held up a leopard print stiletto. "It's classy. Women don't have class anymore. Are you going to get in the car or wait until someone drives by and kills us?"

"I guess I'll get in," Kate said, giving me a look that didn't bode well for me later. "I wouldn't want y'all to have all the fun without me. Nick's going to love this, by the way."

"I figured we could keep this part of the trip to ourselves," I said.

"Secrets kill marriages," Kate said.

"That's true," Angelica said. "Secrets and going

to federal prison. It's hard to have a marriage with either."

"What did you mean when you said you told Vince to let sleeping dogs lie?" I asked. "Did you and Vince have a relationship?"

"You are funny, Double Tap," she said, not answering the question. Then she turned and looked at Kate in the back seat. "Everyone in the mob has nicknames, did you know this?"

"I wasn't aware," Kate said.

"I'll call you Chica," Angelica said. "You are cute and sassy. Double Tap looks like someone has been sucking her blood. I knew a man who used to do that. You have no color in your face. You have dark circles beneath your eyes, and you've chewed your lipstick off."

"Now you sound like my mother," I said. "I told you I'm pregnant. *And* you're holding a gun on me. I'm sorry I'm not looking my best while my life is hanging in the balance."

"Drama llama," Angelica said.

Kate nodded. "She's always been like that. Ever since we were little kids."

"You must be having a girl," Angelica said. "I had all sons. They filled me with beauty. Your spawn is sucking the life from you."

"Congratulations on your sons," I said between clenched teeth. "Are you and Vince having an affair or not? Is he here? I just want to get him and go home. That's all."

"Vince would no doubt be an enthusiastic lover, but he is not mine," she said. "And he is not here."

"That's all I needed to know," I said. "How do I get you back home?"

"Keep driving," she said. "It's a nice evening and the sun's still out for a little while longer. I don't see people too much."

"What about your husband?" I asked.

"Which one?" she asked.

Kate stuck her head between the front seats. "How many are there?"

"My first husband is dead," she said. "And then I have another who only exists for the government."

"Luis," I said. "He shows up all over your background check. Everything is in his name. Even the house."

"Yes," she said. "If ever you need to disappear get the government to give you a fake husband and make you the beneficiary of all his assets. They'll even pay you a monthly stipend for the rest of your life."

"Wow," I said. "How do I get that job?"

"You have to send everyone you love to prison," she said. "It is not as terrible as it sounds if your relatives are horrible people. Now you will answer my questions. How did you find me?"

I figured it was only fair since she'd answered mine and somehow managed to make me more confused than I was when we started.

"Your number was on a napkin from the Four Seasons in Vince's pocket," I said.

"Yes, that's where we agreed to meet for lunch," she said. "He checks up on me from time to time, and he is a man of honor. He can be trusted."

Kate hit me on the back of the shoulder and I winced. "My mother said that Vince has been acting strange lately—distant. And I guess when she found your name and number on that napkin in his pocket she figured you were the reason."

"I agree," she said, pressing her lips together. "That looks bad. We should have tacos and funnel cakes and beer down by the peer. They have outdoor dancing when it gets dark."

"Oh good," Kate said, catching my panic-stricken gaze in the rearview mirror. "Addison was just saying how she wanted tacos."

"Addison?" Angelica asked.

"That's my name," I said.

"It's ridiculous," she said, flapping her hand.

"Anyway," I said. "No one has seen or heard from Vince in three days. And I think he could be in trouble. It looks like he might have been digging into a case he and my father had worked years ago."

"Your father?" she asked.

"Charlie Holmes," I said.

"Sí, sí," she said, clapping her hands together. "Carlos and Vinny. Vince was fire and Carlos was ice. Back in those days I wouldn't have turned down a po-po sandwich."

"Gross," I said, squenching my face. Thinking of my dad in any kind of sandwich wasn't settling well with my digestive system.

I had no idea where I was going. I was driving the coast road back toward the hotel, and I figured she'd tell me where to stop.

"Because I'm good at my job and can put all the clues together pretty easily," Kate said, "I'm going to assume you know something about the old case Vince was looking into. And I'm also going to assume it has something to do with you since you're in WITSEC."

"We have a saying in Puerto Rico. Gato con guantes no caza ratones."

"Yes," Kate said, nodding her head.

"Anyone want to fill me in?" I asked.

"The literal translation means a cat with gloves can hunt no mice," Kate said.

"Right," I said. "That makes no sense."

"It means sometimes you have to get your hands dirty to get the job done right," Angelica said. "And I was the one who got my hands dirty and cleaned up the mess. Your father and Vinny helped me when I didn't think anyone would. Do you know what it's like to be married to someone with so much power that every move you make is under scrutiny all the time?

"I got to the point where I didn't care if I lived or died. I only wanted out. I only had to sacrifice everyone and everything to do it."

Her emotions were so heavy they filled the whole car, and everyone was silent for a couple of minutes before she spoke again.

"Vinny said your father died. I'm sorry. They

were a good team. I didn't trust cops back then. Still don't. But they had this..." She flapped her hand. "I don't know the right word—charisma—bravísimo—machismo." She touched her fingers to her lips and kissed them. "It was beautiful. They were predators, and they weren't going to let go of Carmen de Salva without a fight. It was very sexy to watch them in action."

"And how were you involved with Carmen de Salva?" Kate asked.

"Valentina de Salva," she said, smiling. "His wife."

"Talk about wiping away your past," I said. "There's nothing in your background check that even remotely suggests you had anything to do with the de Salvas. Your marriage license says you and Luis Vega have been married almost forty years."

"Exactly," she said. "There is no such woman. According to media reports, someone set explosives in Valentina's car and she was blown to smithereens. Not even a tooth left for identification." Angelica gave us a toothy grin.

"Ouch," Kate said.

"I really want to hear more of this story," I said. "But I have to stop and use the bathroom."

"There's the pier just ahead of us," Angelica said. "Park on the other side of the Ferris wheel. No one likes to go over there because that's where they put the dumpsters. But it's the easiest place to get in and out of here if a fight breaks out."

"Does that happen often?" I asked.

"It's Miami," she said. "We fight with everyone. And then we make love. We are very passionate."

"Could we be any farther from the bathroom?" I asked.

"Fresh air is good for the baby," Angelica said. "Chica and I will talk and get tacos and funnel cakes while we wait on you. There are picnic tables down by the waterfront."

"Are we really having dinner with a woman who kidnapped us and whose entire history is a lie?" Kate whispered.

"Don't let her kidnap you," I said, and then ran toward the bathroom.

I wasn't very far before I wished I'd had the good sense to wear Kate's flats. I had no idea what was happening or what had changed, but I'd learned two important things—Vince wasn't a cheater, and he was probably in big trouble. The more information I could find out from Angelica, the better I could help Vince.

I wasn't a fan of outdoor public bathrooms, so I finished quickly and then took full advantage of the hand sanitizing dispenser at the entrance. On my way back to the car, I noticed several kiosks selling sunglasses and souvenirs and all kinds of fried foods. And then I noticed the shadier operations where cars were parked with their trunks popped open. There were some who had wares on display and others who had tables set up to read palms and play three-card monte.

It was there I saw the knockoff purses and

quasi-genuine leather goods. It's like I couldn't help myself. I somehow ended up with a black leather motorcycle jacket that would probably fade the first time it rained, but it looked fantastic with my outfit and added some welcome warmth since it was getting cooler as the sun went down.

It took me a few minutes to find the picnic tables down by the water. Strings of colored lights decorated any available surface, and the smell of fried dough and the oil they used on the Ferris wheel was overpowering.

"Did you buy a jacket?" Kate asked once I found them.

"From the guy selling out of his trunk," I said. "He's got all kinds of stuff, and he said they're selling like hot cakes. I got the last one of these in my size."

"Yikes," Angelica said. "Did you just fall off the turnip truck?"

"I like to support small businesses," I said primly. "I want to get back to Vince. If he's not with you then I'm afraid he's in trouble. How did he find you?"

"That's part of the agreement with witness protection," she said. "That you'll never have contact with anyone from your former life. I know Vince and your father were working with that FBI task force, and I have a contact at the FBI if my past comes back to bite my ass. But I never trusted him or those other two cops. Not like Vinny."

"What other two cops?" I asked.

Angelica waved her hand away and said, "I don't remember their names. But they wanted me to fry right along with Carmen, so good riddance to them. Vinny and your dad were the only ones I could trust. So I broke the rules. I sent Vinny and your dad a card with my number and my new name and told them I felt better knowing they would maybe look into it if something happened to me."

I decided to start with the funnel cake instead of the tacos because I'm an adult and can eat dessert first if I want to, and then I asked Angelica, "Did y'all stay in touch a lot over the years?"

"No," she said. "He'd check in every few years. And I'd check in with him if I moved or anything like that. Maybe five or six times we spoke over the last twenty years. I grew up in Miami, so when I had the chance to start a new life and come home, I took it. You have no idea what it's like for a Puerto Rican woman who's married to a mob boss while living in Savannah. That place is *not* my style. I hated every breath I took there. But that's where the money was," she said, shrugging. "And I like money. And I liked the house okay, but the Feds seized all that when they arrested Carmen."

"No one from the FBI found out you and Vince were in contact?" Kate asked.

"Pssh, please," she said. "The FBI don't care about me or Vince. He was just a local cop to them. But he and your daddy did all the work so far as I could see. They actually listened to me. The FBI gave me this new face and a new identity, but Vinny gave me respect."

"I'm more interested to know how you didn't end up in prison," Kate said. "I've read those case files forward and backward. Your nickname was Reina in the de Salva organization."

"What's that mean?" I asked.

"Queen," Kate answered. "So I wonder how you managed to escape a life in prison, while your husband and two of your sons went to federal prison."

Angelica smiled, her black eyes sparkling with good humor. "I knew I liked you. And I think you know the answer."

"You turned your husband over to the Feds," Kate said. "Gave them their case in exchange for your freedom and protection."

"Whoa," I said. "You sent your husband and most of your family to prison and you didn't move to Alaska or the North Pole? How are you not terrified they'll find you?"

She shrugged. "What are they going to do to me from prison?" she asked. "Besides, I'm not without my own resources and security. I'm well protected. I saw the two of you coming from a mile away, and still got the drop on you."

"That's true," Kate said. "You called Vince, didn't you? He wouldn't have come unless you'd needed him. And you've not stopped scanning this place since we got here. You're nervous and you wanted us to all be in public. Why?"

"Me, nervous?" Angelica asked, putting a hand to her chest. "I've never been nervous a day in my life."

"I didn't peg you for a liar," Kate said, and then the tension in the car skyrocketed and I wondered why Kate was antagonizing the woman with the gun. And then I remembered that Kate had a gun too inside her purse, though I was hoping the two women didn't have a showdown in public on the pier. This looked like the kind of place where everyone was armed.

Angelica sighed. "Fine," she said. "And nobody likes a know-it-all. I've felt eyes on me the last couple of months. I haven't seen anyone, but something I learned while being married to Carmen was you always listened to your instincts. There's no new neighbors on my street. No daily joggers I don't recognize. When I'm in my car and feel as if someone is following me I'll watch the cars behind me, but they always turn off."

"Carmen died a couple of months ago in prison," Kate said. "Did your instincts start tingling before or after?"

She narrowed her gaze in thought. "After."

"What about your sons? Do you ever hear from them?"

Her smile was sad. "No, never. They were loyal to their father. They didn't understand why we had to stop."

"Why did you stop it?" I asked. "You had everything you could ever want?"

"All good things must come to an end, sí? We would not have lasted much longer where we were. There is always someone younger and hungrier who wants what you have. Our home base was in Savannah because it was easy and ripe for the taking. But it was also easy access to surrounding states and the gulf."

"You mean drugs?" Kate asked. "Everything is easily transported along the waterways and through the bayous. Drugs have always been a problem in Savannah. From what I remember about the case, your husband insisted he had no idea about the drugs coming into the city."

"No," she said. "Carmen did not have that much ambition to run drugs. He said it was too messy and the stakes of getting caught were too high. You see, Carmen was twenty years older than I was when we married, and he was very set in his ways. He enjoyed his businesses, and they were comfortable and profitable for him. He had influence and power and money. It was enough."

"But it wasn't for you?" I asked.

"I believe in diversifying," she said. "But he had the final say in the matter so I left it alone. And sure enough, someone starts moving in on his territory. A couple of our guys turn up with their throats slit. My youngest son wasn't involved in the business. Alex was going off to college to make something of himself." She smiled, the memories obviously fond. "The police said he was killed in a drive-by, and that he was just in the wrong place at the wrong time. But I knew it was a hit job.

"I could tell Carmen was worried after that, and I just didn't care anymore," she said. "Alex was my only son who didn't make me feel like a failure as a mother. My other boys were very much like their father, only they didn't have Carmen's patience and work ethic."

It was hard to think of a mob boss as having patience and a good work ethic, but I guess it took all kinds.

"Who moved in on your husband's territory?" Kate asked. "As far as I could tell from the reports I read, everyone was convinced it was your husband running drugs. And if I'm not mistaken, the problem disappeared after he went to prison."

"It wasn't Carmen," she insisted. "I'm telling you, I knew everything about our business. Carmen talked everything over with me and there were no secrets. We had a mutual respect for each other and the business."

"Until you sent him to prison," I said.

Angelica shrugged. "He should've listened to me. I was trying to save our family. We all would have ended up like Alex eventually. We had enough money and property. We could've gone anywhere and stayed safe and been together. But Carmen let my boys talk him into staying and fighting back for what was ours. It was a foolish mistake."

I didn't know how I felt about Angelica. I could understand a woman who would fight for her family.

But I couldn't understand a woman who could just sentence them to life if they went against her wishes. It's not like they weren't all criminals, so she couldn't play the righteous card.

"How long ago did you contact Vince about your instincts?" I asked.

"Not long after it started happening," she said. "I told him what was happening. He told me to see if I could verify or get a visual on anyone. He said he was going to make some calls and that was that. Then he calls me a few days ago and says he's flying in and that he's staying at the Four Seasons."

"What'd he tell you?" Kate asked.

"That he'd gotten remarried," she said, smiling slyly. "A girl's gotta try."

"Anything about the case?" Kate asked.

"He said he called the warden where Carmen and my boys are, he said up until his death Carmen ran a pretty tight ship. Carmen has always been a leader of men. They look up to him and would follow him anywhere. Putting him in prison wouldn't have changed that."

"Maybe everyone has left you alone up to this point because Carmen loved you enough to make sure you were taken care of," I said. "And when he died then all bets were off."

She sucked in a breath and held it, thinking about what I'd just said. "I guess that's a possibility. Carmen did love me. But as far as I know, he's always thought me to have died in that explosion. He never knew I betrayed him."

"I wouldn't bet on that," Kate said.

"Carmen had only one visitor since November of last year," Angelica said.

"Who was it?" I asked.

"I don't know," she said, shrugging. "But I'd like to know."

CHAPTER TWELVE

By the time Kate and I had dropped Angelica back off at her house and driven all the way back to our hotel, it felt like the longest day in existence, and it wasn't even eight o'clock yet. All I wanted to do was go upstairs to the room, take my shoes off, and go to bed.

But plans had a way of changing, especially when Scarlet was involved. She was holding court in the lobby when we walked in. The longer I stood there, the less I was sure if she was holding court or if she was just a tourist attraction.

"Why is Scarlet dressed like Elton John at the Ice Capades?" Kate asked.

"I'm assuming she's going full-out Miami," I said.

Scarlet was wearing a tangerine-colored spandex bodysuit with bell-bottom legs and sleeves, and it had a sweetheart neckline that was obviously meant to display massive cleavage—if you happened to

have massive cleavage. Scarlet's cleavage was somewhere around her belly button, so it wasn't quite the
same effect. Her hair was from the Shakira collection and trailed down her back in frosty curls. If you
saw her from the neck up and from the back, she
was a dead ringer.

A couple of people took pictures as they walked
by, and I gave up and took my shoes off right there
in the lobby.

"Where have you girls been?" Scarlet asked. "I
woke up and found your note, and then it took me
all this time to get ready and you still weren't back."

"We got kidnapped," Kate said. "Kind of. It was
a weird afternoon."

"Do I smell funnel cakes?" Scarlet asked,
narrowing her eyes at me.

"That's where the kidnapper took us," I said. "It
wasn't our choice."

"*Hmmph,*" Scarlet said. "Well, I guess if you
didn't have a choice, you didn't have a choice. That's
a real nice jacket. I saw one just like it while I was
walking down to see the sights. This nice man was
selling them out of the back of his trunk. It was a
real good price too. Twenty bucks. Almost bought
one, but he said some skank had just bought the last
one in my size."

"Twenty bucks?" I said. "I paid a hundred."

"There's a sucker born every minute," Scarlet
said. "What's the plan. Dinner? Drinks? Dancing? I
learned how to floss and I want to give it a try."

"I need to call Nick and fill him in," I said. "I'm

uneasy knowing Vince was here, especially if Angelica is being followed. Whoever was trailing her could've latched on to Vince."

"And I'll call Savage and see what he can find out about whoever visited Carmen in prison," Kate said. "And I can get him to start doing a trace on his cell phone to see what tower was pinged last."

"Y'all can do all that at dinner," Scarlet said. "I'm starving and I didn't get all dressed up for nothing. If we eat in the hotel restaurant maybe you can see if anyone recognizes Vince. I thought you said he met Angelica here."

"Good idea," I said. I looked down at the three of us, Kate in red, me in yellow, and Scarlet in tangerine, and thought we looked like we belonged on top of Carmen Miranda's head. Kate must've had the same thought because she just closed her eyes and shook her head.

"Whatever happens on this night," Kate said. "Please don't take any pictures."

I smiled tightly and I ushered Scarlet toward the dining room. It was at the front of the hotel on the first level, and it overlooked the beach.

I didn't actually have a picture of Vince by himself, so I texted my mother and asked if she could send me one. This, of course, led to a couple thousand texts of her asking me if I'd found out anything.

The waiter seated us out on the balcony in a dark corner, but Scarlet wasn't having any of that.

"No, young man," she said. "We'll take that table

right there. I can't read the menu in the dark. Besides, I like how my earrings sparkle under this light."

The maître d' took it in stride and seated us directly in the center of the balcony, under a cacophony of twinkle lights, that did, indeed, make Scarlet's earrings look like disco balls.

"At least it's quiet out here," Kate said.

"Order me something to drink and something that involves a lot of cheese for an appetizer," I told Scarlet. "I'm going to call Nick." I saw the gleeful look in her eye and figured it was worth a reminder. "Nothing alcoholic to drink for me."

"People used to drink all the time when they were pregnant back in the old days, and it never hurt anybody. That was a generation that went off to war and knew how to defend their liberty. Women stopped drinking and now look what we've got—stunted men in suspenders with beards who drink coffee all day and watch porn because they don't know how to flirt with women in real life. I say it's time to take a stand and bring back the greatest generation."

"Maybe you should write a letter to your congressman," I told her. "They love to get suggestions."

"Good idea," she said.

I walked over to the railing and looked out over the dark ocean. The waves crashed gently, and I inhaled the scent of salt and sea as I dialed Nick and waited for him to answer.

"How's Miami?" he asked when he answered.

"I'm not sure," I said. "Scarlet's dressed like Elton John and I got kidnapped and taken for tacos. And Scarlet is trying to get me to drink so we'll give birth to the next greatest generation."

"Maybe you should stay away from Scarlet," Nick said. "Do I want to ask about the kidnapping?"

"Probably not," I said. "But guess who Angelica is."

"I'm on pins and needles," he said.

"Valentina de Salva."

"You're joking," Nick said. "She died in an explosion twenty years ago."

"Nope, she's the one who flipped on her husband and sons and sent them to prison. In exchange, she got WITSEC and a face-lift. Vince and Dad worked that case with the federal task force."

"This is not good," Nick said. "Vince shouldn't be involved with anyone from WITSEC. Why would he do that?"

"Angelica said she didn't trust her FBI contact, so she's kept contact with Vince and Dad all these years. I know Vince was looking into the case. I found a file folder in Dad's shed with all his case notes and more of a journal as he worked the case. Not anything formal."

"You only found one folder?" he asked.

"Yeah, in the top drawer of his file cabinet. I followed the dust trail and saw that's where Vince had been poking around."

"I can promise you he's got more than one file folder," Nick said. "He and Charlie worked on that case for two years. He should have closets of files."

"Or a storage locker?" I asked.

"Or a storage locker," Nick said. "Did you find a storage locker?"

"Scarlet did," I said. "I think I found the key to the lock with the de Salva file."

"I've got an uneasy feeling about this," Nick said. "It all feels wrong. Vince shouldn't be involved with a woman who got immunity and a free pass for the crimes she committed along with her husband. She's a murderer. So don't let her take you for tacos again. I need some Tums."

I swallowed and felt lightheaded. I could have used a couple of Tums myself. "She's a murderer? But she seemed nice. Crazy," I said. "But nice."

"Just be careful," he said. "And stay in contact."

"Kate's talking to Savage to see if he can get a ping from Vince's cell phone. We know he made it back home after he met with Angelica because Edna next door saw him leaving three days ago. He said he was going fishing."

Nick snorted. "Yeah, right," he said. "It sounds like your work in Miami is done. I'll feel better once you're out of there."

"We're flying back out tomorrow," I said. "Are you at home?"

I'd totally forgotten about Rosemarie and Suzanne and the house renovations.

"No, I'm too chicken," he said. "I figured I'd just work all night and sleep at my desk."

"We still own the little house across from Savage. The bed is made, but there's no groceries. I figure we'll have to stay there for a while until we have to have the house condemned or they actually finish the project. The key is under the fake rock."

"Very original," Nick said.

I told him I loved him and then headed back to the table. Kate and Scarlet had a row of shot glasses filled to the brim with a yellow liquid.

"You're not drinking," Scarlet said. "So I split yours up between the two of us."

"It's the responsible thing to do," Kate said, looking very relaxed.

"Before you get too relaxed," I said, "why don't you tell me what Savage said."

Scarlet pushed one of the shot glasses across the table and Kate picked it up. Neither of them bothered with the salt or limes sitting in front of them, and they tossed back the drinks like water.

"I learned to drink during the war," Scarlet said. "I had to build up my tolerance so the Nazis would pass out before I did. You know the saying *'Loose Lips Sink Ships'*? There's a reason for that."

"And how many ships did you sink?" Kate asked.

"Thirty-two," Scarlet said. "I was a very good spy."

"You should write your memoirs one day," Kate said. "I bet you've got dirt on everyone."

"Heh," Scarlet said, taking another shot. "I've got dirt on every head of state and president for decades. Bunch of old pervs. I won't tell you which one, because I want you to buy my book I just decided I'm going to write. But there's a certain president who had elephantine balls. Had to have his pants special made, and one time he sat down wrong and was in the hospital for a week. Fabulous lover though, as long as he didn't take you from behind. Talk about wrecking balls."

Kate choked on her tequila and covered her face with her napkin, and I noticed the people sitting closest to us had stopped their conversation to eavesdrop.

"Kate," I said. "You were telling me about Savage."

"He said he's feeling a lot better and someone made an offer on his house. Looks like he'll be out of there in the next couple of weeks once the doctors release him."

"That's a fine hunk of man," Scarlet said.

"Amen," Kate said.

"Kate," I hissed. "You're a married woman."

"Oh, please," she said. "Don't tell me you didn't take a ride on that merry-go-round when you had the chance. Everyone knows you two had a thing."

I felt the color drain out of my face. "You're joking," I said. "Savage and I never had a fling. What's wrong with you? We just made out a couple of times, and then I felt guilty about it because Nick broke up with me, but I was still thinking about him."

"Wait a second," Kate said, leaning in close across the table. "You're telling me that you had the chance to sleep with Savage, completely free of a relationship with Nick, and you didn't do it? Are you crazy?"

"Maybe she's not a Holmes, after all," Scarlet said, shaking her head. "I always thought your mother showed too much interest in Wally Davis when he delivered the mail. Come to think of it, you kinda look like him around the eyes."

"I do not," I said, glaring at Scarlet. "Mom did not have an affair."

Scarlet *hmmph*ed and pressed her lips together tight, and I looked back at Kate. "Does everyone seriously think Savage and I had a thing?"

"Of course," she said. "You know you can tell us the truth. When you were living outside of the agency in your van, I was still working on a case in the middle of the night. I thought I heard a noise so I looked out the window and your van was rocking so much I thought you might tip over. I saw Savage's truck parked on the other side of the park and put two and two together."

My mouth dropped open. "Ohmigosh," I said. "Savage must've been watching me to make sure I was okay. It was Nick who was doing the rocking. He'd just come to talk, but it was right after I got my hair cut short, and he couldn't help himself. That's really embarrassing. Poor Savage."

"Don't worry about Savage," Kate said. "He'll find another horse to break in."

"I'm not sure I'm comfortable with that analogy," I said. "And as glad as I am that Savage sold his house and is moving on, maybe you could tell me what he said about the case."

"Oh, right," Kate said. "He didn't really say much of anything. Just a lot of grunts. He bet me fifty bucks Scarlet has a weapon on her. And how getting tied up with anyone from the de Salva organization was bad business, whether they're in WITSEC or not."

"Yeah, that was pretty much Nick's take too," I said. Then I turned to Scarlet. "Do you have a weapon on you?"

"It's my constitutional right as an American," she said. "Besides, the guy felt real bad he didn't have a leather jacket in my size, so he gave me a two-for-one special. I got an Uzi and a can of Mace for a good price. He said the Uzi was gently used. That man was a real entrepreneur."

"That's fifty bucks wasted," Kate said.

"I can't believe you took the bet," I said. "Talk about suckers. Finish what you were saying about Savage."

"He's going to try to find out who was visiting Carmen. They'll have to have surveillance. Those aren't as easy to erase without someone losing their job over it. He also said he'd get Vince's last known location. He'll get back with us once he's got something."

"Mom sent me a current picture of Vince," I said, opening the picture on my phone and setting it on the table. "We can ask the manager or anyone here if they remember seeing Vince earlier in the week."

About that time, the waiter showed up to take our order. He was tall and whip lean with skin the color of dark coffee and a smile that lit up the room.

"I'm Sam," he said to me, since he'd obviously already introduced himself to Scarlet and Kate. "I can mix up lots of nonalcoholic drinks for you. The fruit is real good for the baby. Make sure you're taking your prenatal vitamins. You're looking a little pale. Must be having a girl."

I growled and shot Kate and Scarlet a knowing glare.

"We didn't say a word," Scarlet said. "We're innocent."

"Yeah, right," I said, waving my phone.

Sam took one look at the picture of Vince and gasped.

"You recognize him?" I asked.

"Of course," Sam said. "Mr. Walker was a guest earlier this week. Tragic. We at the Four Seasons don't condone that type of behavior, and we wish Mr. Walker the best."

"What behavior?" I asked.

"What happened?" Kate asked.

"Can you bring another round of shots on your way back?" Scarlet asked. "With some chips and salsa."

"Oh," Sam said. "I saw his picture and thought

you were reading the story in the paper. It's been all the rage this week."

"The paper," I said, looking at Kate. "Who would've thought to check the paper?"

"Mr. Walker is a friend of ours and he went missing," Kate said. "We were hoping someone might have seen him."

"Not since the shooting," Sam said. "But that's understandable considering things were chaos at the time."

"There was a shooting?" I asked.

"Yep, right here as a matter of fact," he said. "You can still see the bullet holes in the wall." He pointed behind him, and sure enough, there were three distinct bullet holes in the plaster.

"Oh, God," I said. "I knew something had happened to him."

"He didn't get shot or nothing," Sam said. "The police keep the beaches real safe, but every once in a while there's a lunatic who's had too much to drink and you'll hear shots fired. Poor Mr. Walker was just in the wrong place at the wrong time, and one of the bullets shattered the glass in Mr. Walker's hand. He had to get stitches. The manager comped his room and everything."

"I can imagine," I said. "Was Mr. Walker having dinner with anyone or was he alone?"

"He was alone this time," Sam said. "I'd served him earlier in the day and a woman joined him for lunch."

"Must have been Angelica," Kate said.

"Yes," Sam said, snapping his fingers. "That was her name. Lovely woman."

"Uh-huh," I said. "How many days was Mr. Walker here?"

"He stayed two nights and ate all his meals here in the restaurant. I tried to give him tips for good clubs and the sights around Miami, but he said he was here on business and didn't have time for any fun. I told him to stay out of Vegas because he was so unlucky."

"Because of getting shot at?" Kate asked.

"That, and because he almost got hit by a car earlier that day," Sam said. "He was pretty banged up from that when he came to dinner. His hands were all scraped and the side of his face was all bruised." He pointed to his cheekbone. "I told him he should've ordered room service and an ice pack, but he just laughed and said a good meal and moving around was the best thing for it."

"Nobody saw who almost hit him?" I asked.

"Oh, sure," Sam said. "Lots of people saw. But this is Miami and sometimes the traffic laws aren't always understandable. It happened right after lunch with Ms. Angelica. I heard the squeal of tires and all the screams. Of course, everyone went running to see what happened. And there was Mr. Walker lying on the ground next to the fountain. I ran over and helped him up, but he said he was fine."

"Where was Angelica?" I asked.

"She'd already left in her own vehicle," Sam said.

"I saw a bright yellow Corvette speeding away after all the screams started, and a couple of other people said they saw the Corvette squeal around the corner just as Mr. Walker was walking across to the beach. They said the Corvette never put on the brakes and Vince barely jumped out of the way in time. It's just bad luck all around."

"Yeah, bad luck," I said softly.

When Sam left to get our food, I looked at Scarlet and Kate and said, "We need to find Vince fast. If he got out of here alive it was just by luck. I'm going to call Nick and see if he can get us in touch with the cop who was assigned the case when Vince was shot at. Maybe they've got some more information or know who it was."

"You think Angelica is involved?" Kate asked.

"I think she's in the middle of it," I said. "Whether she's involved or not, I don't know. But I don't think she can be trusted."

CHAPTER THIRTEEN

The next morning, "Bad Boys" woke me from a fitful sleep. Scarlet's snoring the night before had been worse than normal, and we could hear it through the wall. And Kate spent a good portion of the night throwing up her bad decisions. She finally stopped moaning around five in the morning, and I was able to fall asleep.

I reached around on the nightstand and picked up the phone. Kate didn't even make a sound at the intrusion she was sleeping so hard.

"'ello," I croaked.

"Good morning, sunshine," Nick said.

"Don't remind me."

"Sounds like you had a crazy Miami night," he said. I could hear the laughter in his voice.

"Not me," I said. "I was responsible. I came back to the room after dinner. But Crockett and Tubbs decided to hit the town after doing shots.

Scarlet came back to the room with Kate draped around her, drunk as a skunk. Kate paid for it all night and I had to listen to it."

"What about Scarlet?" Nick asked.

"Like she never had a drop to drink," I said. "Her stomach and liver must be made of cast iron."

"Well, rise and shine," Nick said. "It's almost noon and y'all are supposed to fly back this afternoon. I don't like sleeping alone."

"I'm not too fond of it either," I said.

"I got in touch with Miami PD this morning," Nick said. "Detective Ryan Orlando is your contact. He's expecting you."

"Wow, thanks," I said. "Being married to a cop comes in handy sometimes."

"I live to serve," he said. "Hurry back. Someone delivered a NAD Squad shirt to the door dressed like Gandalf. Scared the hell out of me."

"I'm impressed you know who Gandalf is," I said. "You're a closet nerd."

"Hush, and get home quick. The neighbors are creeping me out."

He hung up and I rolled to the edge of the bed and put my feet on the floor. I was expecting the nausea to come, just like it did every morning, but I felt...good. I got out of bed and showered and dressed with an extra pep in my step.

When I came out of the bathroom, Kate was still fast asleep. I went over and held my finger under her nose to make sure she was still breathing, and satisfied, I knocked on the connecting door between my and Scarlet's rooms.

She pulled the door open, and never in a million years would I have guessed she'd spent the night drinking and dancing. She was up and dressed in another tracksuit, this one yellow with rainbow-striped piping, and her bright white shoes. Her hair was short and hot pink today.

"Nice hair," I said. "Whose is it?"

"Madonna," she said. "That Shakira hair gave me a headache. Besides, I gave it to some nice man named Tony last night. He really admired it, and I like to donate to the arts."

"I didn't think you'd be awake," I said.

"Been up a couple of hours. I was just coming to get you to see if you wanted breakfast. I ordered enough for all of us."

I stepped into the room and the smell of cooked meat assaulted me. I slapped a hand over my mouth and ran back to the bathroom.

"Does that mean you don't want breakfast?" I heard Scarlet yell through the bathroom door.

Half an hour later, I made a second attempt at leaving the room. Scarlet had finished breakfast and Kate was buried under the covers with her pillow on top of her head.

"Never met a Holmes who couldn't hold her bacon," Scarlet said.

"I think this baby is trying to kill me."

"Now that sounds like a Holmes," she said. "What are we doing today?"

"We're going to the police station," I said. "Leave your Uzi here."

"You're no fun," she said. "What if we get in a gun fight?"

"Then the hundreds of cops surrounding us will protect us with their guns," I said.

Scarlet snorted. "Shows what you know."

After I checked Scarlet for weapons, we took an Uber to the police station. It was a huge white building of modern architecture and curves and windows. We made our way to the front desk and I asked for Detective Orlando and gave my name and ID. No one asked for Scarlet's ID, which I was grateful for. I was pretty sure she was still wanted for questioning in Ugly Mo's murder, and she did have that restraining order in Miami. There was no telling what her police record looked like, and in hindsight, I probably should've left her at the hotel. It was like waving a red flag in front of a bull.

"Man, did this place get a face-lift since the last time I was here," she said.

"And there you go," I said, figuring I was right to worry.

The sergeant at the front desk directed us to the second floor, and we got on an elevator crowded with cops and a guy in cuffs who smelled like he hadn't had a bath in the last year.

"These cops get younger every year," Scarlet whispered. "That fella there doesn't look old enough to drive. How's he able to carry a gun and I can't?"

"Because he's a cop," I told her.

"I could be a cop if I wanted, but they got age discrimination," she said. "What's the smell? Is that me?"

"It's not you," I said, holding my breath. I was pretty sure my stomach couldn't get emptier than it was, but I didn't want to take a chance, especially in an elevator full of people.

When the elevator doors opened, everyone rushed out in a *whoosh*, and Scarlet and I followed behind them to a big open area that was loud and chaotic, with rows of desks and glass partitions. The view from the second floor showed a view of downtown Miami and palm trees. All in all, I wouldn't have minded seeing that view every day.

There was a man standing in the middle of the aisle. He was a couple of inches taller than me and maybe a decade older. He was Hispanic and his hair was speckled with silver. He wore loose linen pants in khaki and a matching suit jacket in silk with the sleeves rolled up. His badge hung around his neck from a gold chain and I could see his weapon under the jacket.

Scarlet elbowed me in the side. "It's just like *Miami Vice* up in here," she hissed. "Look at that woman's shoes. Completely impractical if you've got to run down a perp. Lordy, why is that handsome man staring at us like that? He is good looking, and he doesn't look like an infant like those cops downstairs. They must put all the seasoned cops on the second floor. You think he's married?"

"Does it matter?" I asked, curious.

"Of course," she said. "I'd never lure a married man away from his wife. Now, if a man decided to leave his wife for me then I'm in the clear and that's on him."

"Huh," I said. "Detective Orlando?"

I reached out my hand to shake his outstretched one, and he smiled in greeting. "You must be Addison Holmes. I talked to your husband this morning." Then he turned to Scarlet. "And who might you be?"

"You can call me Betty," Scarlet said. "That was one of my code names during the war. I never tell a handsome man my real name on the first date."

Detective Orlando's smile widened and he said, "Very understandable. There are a lot of scoundrels in the world. Please, come have a seat in my cubicle and I'll try to answer whatever questions you might have."

"You have nice skin," Scarlet said. "Nice and smooth. I like a little diversity in my lineup. Are you married?"

"I am," he said, eyes laughing. "But if I wasn't, I can assure you I'd be happy to be part of your lineup until you would no doubt break my heart." He kissed Scarlet's hand, and I could practically hear her heart flutter.

She gave him a coy look and a wink and then took one of the vacant seats across from his desk.

"Thank you so much for seeing us," I said. "We're heading back home this afternoon, and we just learned what happened at the hotel late last night."

"Yes, it's been a strange week," he said. "That's a nice part of town. Lots of money in the area. Lots of tourism. We keep a high profile so the tourists feel safe. Of course, there's always evil in the world. You can't police it all."

"The man who was shot at, Vince Walker," I said. "He's my stepfather and he's missing. He's a retired cop, and we think he was looking into an old case that might have gotten him in trouble."

Orlando's eyes narrowed sharply. "His case led him here to Miami?" he asked.

"It seems so," I said. I debated how much to tell him. Between Scarlet and my conversation with Angelica, I was becoming paranoid about who could be trusted. "Do you have any idea who could've shot at him?"

Orlando blew out a breath. "Unfortunately, no," he said. "We got conflicting reports from witnesses on what the vehicle looked like, plus it was dark outside. It looked like a drive-by and that your step-father was just in the wrong place at the wrong time. How would they have known he'd be sitting there eating dinner?"

"That's a good point," I said. "And normally, I'd agree, except someone also tried to run him down that afternoon."

Orlando nodded. "I asked him about the scrapes and bruises when I questioned him, and he told me about the car incident. There are people who are just that unlucky."

"He didn't tell you he was a cop," I said.

"No, but he didn't have to," Orlando said. "I could tell he was either a cop or military. I was leaning toward cop. He never broke a sweat. You can imagine what it was like—people screaming and crying, others running for cover and hiding. But he took cover and managed to give me a very detailed report of what happened. According to Vince, it looked like a black sedan that the shooting came from. And from what I understood, it was a yellow sports car that almost hit him earlier in the day."

"Did you follow up with Vince?" I asked.

"He gave me his card and number, but he said he was flying out early the next morning to head home. There wasn't really anything to follow up with, so I didn't speak to him again. We got camera footage, but it's just out of range. We collected the slugs from the wall. We interviewed as many witnesses as we could find. There's really not much else we can do. But I hope you find your stepfather."

"Me too," I said. "Thanks for your time." Scarlet had been eerily quiet during our conversation, and when Orlando went into a coughing fit, I was almost afraid to turn and look at her.

I blew out a sigh of resignation. Scarlet had unzipped the jacket of her tracksuit so her black lacy bra was showing and she was running her finger suggestively across her décolletage.

"Please let me know if you hear anything," I

said, handing him a card of my own. I grabbed Scarlet and pulled her back toward the elevator. I could hear Orlando's laughter until the elevator doors shut.

"These new push-up bras I got off QVC really do the job," she said. "Did you see the look on his face? Speechless. I've still got it."

"Yep," I said. "You haven't aged a day."

CHAPTER FOURTEEN

I ALMOST KISSED THE GROUND WHEN WE ARRIVED back in Savannah.

Kate was still hungover and looked like a zombie, and she'd spent the flight with a mask over her eyes to block out the sunlight. Scarlet had talked nonstop the entire way home, regaling some poor man who'd gotten separated from his wife on the flight about her adventures in Miami and how we'd made her leave her Uzi at the front desk of the hotel to hand over to the police.

By the time we got the van and were headed back into the city, I felt like I'd been flying for hours. I just wanted to go home and crawl into bed. But I couldn't go home, because my home was being torn to pieces by the demolition crew from hell.

Kate and Scarlet both slept on the ride back to Whiskey Bayou. In all honesty, I wasn't quite sure what to do with Scarlet. There was no way she could stay with us in the little house across from Savage.

At least not without the whole neighborhood trying to burn us down because of her snoring.

When we pulled up to Kate's house, I helped her get inside and left her on the couch with an ice pack and a bottle of aspirin. When I got back out to the van, Scarlet was wide awake, her Madonna wig sticking up on one side from where she'd been sleeping, and she'd found a pack of pork rinds she'd bought at the airport in her bag.

"I'm starving," she said. "Maybe your mother has sandwich fixins."

The last thing I wanted to do was stop by my mother's because I'd have to fill her in on what had happened. But I also knew that if it was me in her position and no one kept me up to date, the wrath of Godzilla would have nothing on me as I destroyed everyone in my path.

"She always has something to eat," I said. "Let's go give her the news."

"What news?" Scarlet asked.

"About Vince."

"Ahh, yes," Scarlet said. "Maybe we should get a sandwich and run. I can't handle a lot of drama today. Miami was more than I could handle. I remember why I'm not supposed to enter the city limits anymore."

"I thought you just had a restraining order for that one club," I said, looking at her, appalled. "What could you have possibly done to get kicked out of an entire city?"

"Eh," she said, waving her hands. "I was set up.

And no one even recognized me because I was wearing a disguise."

"We walked right into the police station," I said between gritted teeth. "What if they'd arrested you?"

Scarlet snickered. "That's what makes it such a rush. I walked right under their noses. I'm slippery as an eel. Always have been, always will be."

I was going to park in the driveway next to the General Lee, but my car was still there from when Scarlet had absconded with it. That seemed like ages ago.

"Look at old Edna Mohlner," Scarlet said. "I bet she's got blisters in her fingers from hanging on to that fence and peeping over. She always was a snoop. Never liked her, even when she was a kid."

We got out of the van and went in the back way to the kitchen door.

"Why, Edna," Scarlet said. "Did you get your hair done? It looks lovely. Takes twenty years off."

I looked behind me to make sure I wasn't having any out-of-body experience, but Scarlet really was giving Edna a compliment. Her smile was as fake as could be, and her fingers were crossed behind her back. Edna patted her freshly styled hair and preened a little.

"Just got it done today," Edna said. "Jolene said it's all the rage. You know how these styles circle back into popularity. Still haven't seen hide nor hair of Vince. Something must be going on. Did he walk out on Phyllis? Someone mentioned it at the Piggly

Wiggly the other day, but I told them straight out Vince would never do such a thing. He's pined for her forever, and he's just not the type of man to get what he wants and then throw it away. So I figure it's probably Phyllis's fault. She always has had a hot temper. Lord, I could hear her and Charlie screaming at each other from time to time. Sometimes it got so bad I'd just bring my lawn chair to the back porch and listen to the show. It was like the old radio broadcasts when I was a kid."

My patience with Edna was running thin, so I figured it was imperative to make a hasty exit.

"Good to see you, Ms. Edna," I said.

"I was just lying about her hair," Scarlet whispered from the side of her mouth. "Sometimes you've got to butter people up so they'll do things for you later. But between you, me, and the fencepost, she looks an awful lot like that *Tiger King* fella."

I snorted out a laugh and we walked into my mother's kitchen. She must've heard us drive up, because she was already at the counter making sandwiches.

"You need to feed my granddaughter," my mother said. "You look terrible."

"I think that has more to do with my roommates than the baby," I said. "Scarlet and Kate painted the town red last night."

"I thought you weren't supposed to go to Miami anymore?" she asked Scarlet.

"What they don't know, won't hurt them,"

Scarlet said. "I'd like extra pickles. I'm feeling a little vitamin deficient today."

Scarlet scooted onto the bench in the small kitchen nook, her feet not even touching the floor.

"So?" my mother asked. "What did you find out about Vince? Whatever it is, I can take it. Was it another woman? It was, wasn't it? Was she beautiful?"

"Of course she was beautiful," Scarlet said. "It's Miami. Everyone in Miami is beautiful."

"Vince isn't having an affair," I said quickly, shooting Scarlet a narrowed glare. She just shrugged her shoulders and straightened her wig as she looked at the compact from her purse.

"He's not? Well, did you find him? What's wrong with him if he's not having an affair?"

"From what I can find out, he's working an old case he and Dad had about twenty years ago, and the woman Angelica was an informant of sorts."

"Why wouldn't he just tell me that?" she asked.

"Maybe because the last time they poked into this case the police had to drive by our house on a rotation to make sure no one killed us."

She raised her brows and her cheeks turned red. "Do not tell me that man is poking around in the de Salva case again," she said, whacking her spoon on the bowl where she'd been mixing up her special sandwich spread.

She was angry. And I couldn't remember the last time I saw my mother angry. She usually tried to handle things with breathing and yoga and other weird techniques so she could reach zen, but apparently, that was all out the window when it came to the de Salva case.

"I swear if that man brings those criminals back into our lives after everything we went through the last time then he can sleep in the shed like your father did."

"Maybe he knew you'd get mad, so that's why he didn't say anything," I said.

"He's retired," she said, banging the spoon again. At that rate, she was going to shatter the bowl. "He shouldn't be looking into any cases."

"Maybe you're not exciting enough for him," Scarlet said. "He's been a cop his whole life. Maybe you don't live up to the adrenaline rushes he's used to. It's hard for those of us who've constantly put our lives on the line to live a regular life."

"Not helping, Aunt Scarlet," I said, giving her another look.

"You know how these things go," I told Mom. "Sometimes cops get dragged into cases or situations with no provocation of their own. Vince is a good guy. I think you need to give him the benefit of the doubt. We've proven he's not cheating. Let that be enough for now."

"Fine," Mom said. "Then where is he? If he's not sidled up with that hussy Angelica then why isn't he home?"

This was the part I was going to have to fib on. I had no idea where Vince was, and the chances of him being in trouble or dead seemed unreasonably high.

"I'm sure he's on his way home as we speak," I said.

Scarlet went into a fit of coughing and I swore I heard her say, "Liar," over and over again. I went over to pound her on the back and her cough magically disappeared.

My phone rang and I practically ran to answer it before I had to keep lying to my mother. I was praying for any way to get out of this mess.

"Hello," I said.

"Addison, it's Rosemarie," she said. "I'm over at your house, and I'm afraid I need a ride."

"What happened?" I asked.

"Barry and I had a little disagreement about your front porch."

"We don't have a front porch," I said.

"You do now," she said. "It'll look real good in a couple days. If Barry comes back to work."

"Rosemarie," I said. "I don't care what you have to do, you get Barry and his band of merry men back to that house to finish the job, or I'm going to hunt down every one of you and it's not going to be pretty."

I could hear Rosemarie gulp across the line. "Wow, those pregnancy hormones are working a number on you. Maybe you should switch to chamomile tea."

I growled and I grabbed the sandwich my mom had just finished making me and took a huge bite. I figured it was best to shove something in my mouth so I couldn't speak.

"I promise we'll get everything smoothed over and the crew will be back at work bright and early tomorrow morning. But when Barry and I had our disagreement, he loaded up the boys when I went to the bathroom to splash cold water on my face, and they left me here by myself. I was going to just help myself to one of the cars in the garage—really, Addison, I don't see why Nick has to have so many cars. It seems wasteful when it's only the two of you."

"Rosemarie—"

"Anyway," she trilled. "I couldn't find where y'all keep the keys, so if you could come pick me up I'd appreciate it."

I blew out a breath and tried one of those counting exercises my mother swore by. "I'm on the way now," I said. "Meet me at the road. I don't want to see what you've done to the house."

"Oh, good point. I want it to be a surprise."

"Yeah, that's what I meant," I said, hanging up.

"I've got to go pick up Rosemarie," I said, wrapping the rest of my sandwich in a paper towel so I could take it with me.

"I'll come too," Scarlet said. "I don't have anything else to do, and I'm wide awake. Must be the jet lag."

"We didn't cross any time zones," I said.

"We crossed cultures," she said. "That's exhausting. Thanks for the sandwich, Phyllis. I'm sure

Vince is just fine. If he survived the drive-by and the hit-and-run, he can survive anything."

"Wha—" my mother asked, but I was already pushing Scarlet out the back door.

I waited until we were in the van and driving out of town before I asked, "Why do you do that to Mom? I know you do it on purpose. You goad and goad until she explodes or wants to kill you. What's she ever done to you?"

"She married your father," Scarlet said. "And they never would've gotten married if you hadn't been on the way."

I blew out a breath and rolled my eyes. "They were married almost thirty years. One of them always could've left."

"That's their business," Scarlet said. "All I know is they weren't right for each other. And they had ups and downs their whole marriage because of it. Your father, bless him, didn't have an ounce of Holmes in him except for the last name. What a square. I think your mom tried for a while. And then she stopped trying. And then she tried extra hard again."

"What does that mean?" I asked. But it did no good because Scarlet closed her eyes and pretended to sleep the rest of the way to our house.

I saw Rosemarie standing by the road near the mailbox. She was dressed in a blue denim work shirt with the sleeves rolled up, a pair of navy pants stained with paint and plaster, and a red-and-white polka dot bandana.

"Why's she dressed like Rosie the Riveter?" Scarlet asked.

"Oh, you're awake now?" I asked. "How convenient."

Scarlet smiled, and Rosemarie opened the sliding door and got in. "Boy, am I glad to see you girls. What have I missed? I heard you went to Miami. Did you have a good time? Did you go dancing? I always wanted to dance in Miami like JLo."

"It's not as easy as it looks," Scarlet said. "If I didn't have two titanium hips I wouldn't have made it through the night. I'm practically bionic."

"Where am I taking you?" I asked. I just wanted to get rid of everyone in the van and go home to Nick, wherever home was. Though he'd probably be at work for a couple more hours. Really, I just wanted to be in my own space and bask in the peace and quiet.

"Just drop me at the shop," Rosemarie said. "My car is parked there."

"And what about you, Scarlet?" I asked.

"What about me?" she asked.

"Now that the house is under renovation none of us can stay there. You're going to have to find a hotel that hasn't kicked you out. Or maybe you can keep Mom company until Vince comes home."

"That's just cruel, girl," she said. "I don't know. Let me think about it. I'm not used to my own flesh and blood kicking me to the street."

I wondered why my jaw was hurting and then I realized I was grinding my teeth.

"I guess I could always go back to my house, but I don't like it there. I would've sold it a long time ago, but it's been in the family for decades."

"You have your own house?" Rosemarie and I asked together.

"Of course I have my own house. Where do you think I keep all my crap?"

"I did always wonder," Rosemarie said.

We were stopped at a light and my phone rang again. I dropped my head to the steering wheel and banged it a couple of times. I thought it might help the situation, but it turns out, it didn't. Now I had a headache.

"Is this a bad time?" Savage asked.

"I'm not sure," I said. "Do you need an answer right now?"

Savage laughed. "Maybe I can give you some good news."

"Don't tease me like that. It's cruel."

"That must have been a heck of a trip to Miami," he said.

"Don't ask. What's the news?"

"I got a ping off Vince's cell phone," he said. "Looks like he's in the swamps. Do y'all have a fishing camp or anything like that? That's all that's around there."

"My dad had one," I said. "Honestly, I haven't thought about it in years. I've only been there once when I was a kid."

"I'd start there," Savage said. "I'll text you the

location. Or as close to it as I can get you. Addresses aren't really existent out there."

"Great, I appreciate it," I said. "Really."

"Anything for you, kiddo."

"You mean that?" I asked.

"Maybe," he said.

"Maybe Aunt Scarlet could stay with you for a couple of days while the house is being renovated."

"Anything but that," he said and hung up.

CHAPTER FIFTEEN

"Change of plans," I said. "Savage pinged Vince's cell phone to a fishing cabin somewhere in the bayou. I need to go now. If I wait too long it'll be dark and I've never done well in the bayou when it's dark." I shuddered just thinking about it.

Rosemarie nodded. "You remember Kenny Lane and Judy Strand? They went into the bayou 'cause they were afraid Judy's daddy was going to catch them doing the deed. Kenny wasn't the sharpest knife in the drawer and had hidden a pirogue under some tarps. He thought he was being romantic and he put a bunch of pillows and blankets in the bottom of the boat, thinking they'd float out and make love under the moonlight. Well, all he'd really done was make a snake den. They were real comfortable under those blankets until Kenny started pounding away at the poor girl. And when the police found them a few days later they were still joined, only their bodies looked like they'd been sucked dry of fluids. My cousin Ernie was water patrol then, and he quit the next day and went to work at a shoe factory. Said it was the most horrible thing he'd ever seen."

"That's not helping," I said.

"It'll be fine," Rosemarie said. "We'll all go together. You don't need to be by yourself anyway."

As much as I'd wanted to be alone only minutes earlier, I was more than happy to have them along for the trip.

I turned the van around and headed back toward Whiskey Bayou, and then I plugged Savage's directions into the GPS. It would only take me so far, and I was going to have to rely on a childhood memory to get me the rest of the way. The only thing I remembered about the fishing cabin was that it had a green tin roof and matching shutters. My mother had also hung some chimes from the front porch, but they had sounded like ghosts to a seven-year-old girl, and after a weekend of night-mares, my father decided the fishing cabin wasn't for me.

"I just know he's going to be there," Rosemarie said. "I've got real good instincts and I come from a long line of psychics."

My hands were sweating as I turned onto a one-lane swamp road that led deeper into the bayou. There were fishing cabins up closer to the turnoff, but I didn't see any vehicles or boats. And no green roofs.

"I think you're supposed to turn left up here," Scarlet said.

"Are you sure?" I asked, squinting at the GPS.

"Unless I'm reading it upside down," Scarlet said. "But I don't think I am. I've got a real good sense of direction. Take a left."

The main road wasn't the best, and there were narrower roads that snaked off in each direction that led to different camps. I didn't know how far we'd driven along the main road, but I knew there couldn't be too much more road left until we hit swamp, so I did as Scarlet said and took a left.

The road had been partially boarded over so larger vehicles could get through easier, but with as much rain as we'd had the last month, some of the boards had come loose and slid off the road.

"I don't know if this is right," I said, chewing on my bottom lip. "This road is in really bad shape."

"It'll be fine," Scarlet said. "Just drive a little faster so you get good traction and won't be sliding all over the road like you're doing."

That seemed counterintuitive to me. It seemed if you couldn't do something slow, then you probably wouldn't be able to do it fast either. But I pressed down a little harder on the accelerator and the tires spun before they grabbed the road again.

"I think I should go back," I said.

"Going back is for quitters," Scarlet said. "Charge!"

It was too late by then. The muddy, swampy road had taken control of the van, and there wasn't a thing I could do about it but hold on to the wheel like an idiot. We started sliding, and then it was nothing but screams, curses, and a *thunk* from the back when Rosemarie fell onto the floor. We slid off the road and the van plunked into the marsh.

"Everybody out of the van," I said. "I don't know how deep this is."

"It's always been my biggest fear to die in quick-sand," Rosemarie said, throwing open the back door.

"Grab whatever you can carry," I said. "I've got some blankets and an extra coat back there." I hauled Scarlet across my lap and got her out my side and back on solid ground.

"How about that?" Scarlet said. "Turns out you should've gone back the other way."

"Okay," I said. "Here's the deal. You two are going to stay here and try to call for help. No," I said when it looked like Scarlet was going to inter-rupt. "I'm in charge now. Call for help. I'm going to follow the main road while it's still light and see if I can find the cabin. I can move faster without you two."

Scarlet looked like she wanted to interrupt again, but I shot her a look to be quiet.

"Vince has his car. I'll borrow it and then come back and pick the two of you up. It doesn't look like the van is moving any, so just open up the back doors and sit in the back and bundle up while you wait for me. I won't be long."

"Can I say something now?" Scarlet asked.

"Make it quick." I was in no mood for any more of Scarlet's suggestions.

"I just wanted to tell you your pants are unzipped."

I put on my new leather jacket, zipped my pants, and flounced off down the boarded road where we'd come.

Fifteen minutes later, I had to admit defeat. I was lost.

Not only was I lost, but I was lost in the bayou. The bayou had me, and once it had you it would never let you go. I'd give birth alone, surrounded by nothing but swamp and snakes and gators, and I'd raise him to be a hunter and trapper and we'd live in the marsh. They'd tell stories of us in town and we'd become an urban legend. Unless I got eaten by an alligator, leaving my son to fend for himself like Mowgli in *The Jungle Book*.

My GPS was having a stroke and the sexy Australian I'd chosen to give me directions kept saying he was rerouting and that we were going on a walkabout. I was about to throw my phone into the trees when I came upon a road slightly hidden behind overgrown brush. But I could see fairly fresh tire tracks.

I started down the road, walking as fast as I dared so I didn't slip until I came into a clearing. And then I wanted to give a great big shout. In front of me was a tiny fishing cabin with a green tin roof. The cabin was on stilts and there was a bridge that led from the porch, across the marsh, to the levy where Vince's bright red SUV was parked.

I started running, and then I hit a wet patch and I skidded all the way to the bridge post. If I hadn't caught it I would've ended up face-first in the marsh.

The front door opened, and Vince came out onto the porch with a shotgun. His hand was wrapped in a white bandage, and his face was scraped and bruised. He looked like he'd been through the wringer.

"Don't shoot," I said.

"I wasn't sure what was making all that racket," he said. "But it makes sense now."

"Boy, you're in a lot of trouble."

Vince smiled. "I can only imagine. You better get in here and get something warm to drink."

"I can't stay long," I said. "The van slid off the road and Rosemarie and Scarlet stayed with it. I told them I'd borrow your car and pick them up."

Vince nodded. "Keys are in the magnetic box under the tire well."

"That's where Dad used to keep them," I said, remembering fondly. "I don't mean to be rude, Vince, but what the hell were you thinking? We've been looking all over for you. Mom was convinced you were having an affair. I assured her you're not, so she probably won't kill you when you come home."

"I've always enjoyed Phyllis in a temper," he said.

"I'm sure that will be a comfort after the last

month," I said. "I found the file in Dad's shed on the RICO case. And I tracked down Angelica in Miami. Maybe you could fill in some of the blanks for me."

Vince's face went stark white, only emphasizing the cuts and bruises. "You talked to Angelica? Are you out of your mind? Do you know who she is?"

"She told us," I said.

"Us?"

"Me and Kate. We were there together. And Scarlet," I added. "But we left her at the hotel."

"This whole thing is such a mess," he said, running a hand through his hair. "Here, let me put some coffee on while I explain."

I felt bad about telling him I was off coffee, but I wouldn't mind holding a hot cup considering my leather jacket wasn't as warm as it had been in Miami, so I didn't stop him from making it.

"You know about the RICO case?" he asked.

"Yeah, Kate filled me in on a lot of it. And I found out some from Angelica. She's a complicated woman. Crazy. But complicated. Who sends their husband and children to prison on purpose?"

"You don't know the half of it," he said. "I've learned something important over the course of my career."

"What's that?" I asked.

"To never trust anyone," he said. "And when Angelica reached out right after she was put in WITSEC I didn't really have a choice but to play the role she set me up for. You can imagine what it feels like to take down a criminal ring the caliber of de Salva, and know with certainty that the master-mind behind all of it is still roaming the earth free and clear. They didn't call her the queen for nothing. She sent me a handwritten thank-you card with her new name and contact number to my home address. Your dad got one too. She knew everything about us. She mentioned personal things that no one knew. She mentioned you and Phoebe in the letter to your dad.

"After that, all we could do was wait. She wouldn't contact us often, just every few years. But it was often enough to know she was still keeping watch on us. She'd dress it all up in polite speech and thank-yous, and there was nothing ever threatening outright. But you couldn't help but feel threatened."

"Why did she want to keep tabs on you?" I asked.

"Because my team couldn't be bought," he said. "Charlie and I hand selected the cops we trusted to work the case. And the FBI and DEA guys were getting bought off left and right. And the ones who didn't get bought were turning up dead."

"Did it have to do with the drugs that were taking over de Salva's territory?" I asked. "Angelica explained about the competition moving in. She said that's why she sent them to prison. She said whoever was running the drugs would've killed all of them if they'd stayed around much longer."

Vince snorted. "Yeah, well, we were pretty sure

at the time that the drugs were being run by a guy named Rudy Guzman. Very slick. Very polished. Carmen de Salva was rough. He was old school, and he worked the system the old-fashioned way—through hard work and intimidation. But Rudy was a politician. Came out of nowhere. No one knew anything about him—where he was from, what his real name was. All we knew was it wasn't long after he moved to town that the drug problem in Savannah skyrocketed. We felt like idiots chasing our tails. We knew he probably had help from someone high up in the city. But even with the help of someone high up in the city, that didn't explain how he was getting around de Salva."

A little lightbulb was starting to flicker in my brain. "Valentina de Salva," I said.

Vince nodded. "We knew it was her. That's why it made us sick when the Feds agreed to the immunity deal in exchange for her husband and everyone in his organization. She was eliminating the competition. But they just wanted to close a big case and say they brought down the de Salvas. It looked great in the press."

"It's been twenty years," I said. "Why is this all coming back to light now? Angelica is down in Miami. Carmen is dead. Her sons will be in prison for the rest of their lives. What's changed?"

"Carmen was murdered," he said.

"What?" I asked. "How? He was an eighty-year-old man who's been in prison for twenty years."

"Because I was in contact with him before he

died," Vince said. "And I'm telling you, he wasn't your ordinary eighty-year-old man. He was tough and strong and in good health. He ran that prison yard like he was the warden."

"You were the one who's been visiting Carmen in prison?" I asked.

He looked at me as if he'd never seen me before. "Why would you say that?"

"Because Savage checked to see if he'd had any visitors," I said. "And the warden told him he'd only had one visitor, but the logs had disappeared."

Vince blew out a sigh. "Yeah, that cost a pretty penny. I figured it'd buy me a little time before they checked the cameras. There's no way to make those disappear."

"Why were you visiting de Salva?" I asked.

"Because Valentina had help, and it wasn't Rudy Guzman. Guzman was a politician, but he had no brains. There was no way he was smart enough to coordinate drug shipments in and out of different waterways, while avoiding everyone who had them all under surveillance."

"So she had help from cops," I said.

"The guy running the federal task force was a good guy. Agent Simmons. But he must've hit a nerve because he ended up dead, along with the DA and another couple of local cops. They were wiping out anyone who was clean. I think the only reason my team stayed intact was because we were just workhorses. We didn't have any power, and it was never our decision what plan was implemented.

"Your dad was never settled with this case," Vince said. "He was obsessed. But he was like that with cases, so I didn't think anything of it. He and your mom even split up once because he couldn't be anything but a cop."

"I don't remember," I said.

"You were really young," Vince said softly. "I just hadn't realized that he'd kept digging into it all the years before he died."

"Why did you visit Carmen?" I asked.

"Because I found the file in your dad's shed last October," he said. "That's when I decided to go pay a visit to Carmen. I wanted to see what he knew, what he thought." Vince shrugged and brought me a mug of coffee, though I noticed he didn't make one for himself. He was nervous, though he was trying not to let it show.

"What did Carmen say?" I asked, wrapping my cold hands around the mug. I almost moaned at the warmth.

"He was skeptical at first," Vince said. "He remembered me, but he was cool as a cucumber. We didn't talk about much at first, but then I asked him how he felt about what Valentina did to him and his sons and he just smiled. He didn't answer. Just told me he enjoyed our talk and to come back and see him again. So I did.

"When I came back the next time, he was a little more talkative. Told me he'd had a lot of time to think about Valentina, and he didn't hold any grudges against her. She was what she was—a beautiful woman with a calculating mind and no conscience—and he knew that about her when they got married.

"He also knew she was messing around on him with someone, but he figured it all equaled out since he was never faithful to her either. He was a fascinating man. A great storyteller. And it was hard to remember him as the criminal he was."

"Angelica was like that when I talked with her," I said, understanding.

He shook his head. "I still can't believe you went to Miami to see her. You're lucky you're still alive."

"You certainly got lucky," I said.

He nodded. "The last time I talked to Carmen was a day before he died. I don't think that's a coincidence. And he was cremated within hours of his death, before family or anyone else could be notified. He told me on my last visit that he could appreciate a guy like me, who was always on the up and up. He thinks it takes as much skill for a cop to be good as a criminal to be bad. It's probably a closer line than most people know.

"Anyway," Vince said. "Carmen was a showman. He liked to be in control. And even behind bars he wanted to run the show. So he'd feed me a little at a time and then tell me to come back and see him. So that's what I did."

"And then he died," I said.

"And took whatever he was going to tell me to the grave. I knew I was getting close to something. Angelica might have gotten immunity for her crimes, but there are still people out there who she didn't implicate. Like I said, she didn't do it alone. And corruption usually starts at the top. I think Charlie was assembling a list of everyone who was involved, and I think he was going to go after them.

"Every time I read through that file he left in the shed, something about it just didn't feel right. There were sections missing, and sometimes he got a detail wrong about the case. Charlie never got details wrong. And I mean never. The more I read through the file, the more I realized your dad had made that file for me. Almost like a key that only I could understand. I knew he had to have the real files somewhere, but I looked everywhere. They were nowhere in the house, his office, the shed. So I figured he had them off-site."

"In a storage unit," I said.

"You really have become a very good investigator," Vince said. "Your dad would be proud of you."

I don't know why that made me tear up. Maybe it was the hormones. Or maybe because I'd never really known if my dad was proud of me. He was kind of a hard nut to crack.

Vince moved in and took the cooling coffee from me and set it on the table. Then he gave me a hug, and I held on for dear life.

"Sorry," I said a couple of minutes later. I pulled away and wiped my eyes. "I think marriage has made me soft."

Vince's lips twitched. "Believe me, the right

marriage makes you the right kind of soft. You're on the right track, kid."

"What did you find in the storage unit?" I asked.

"I didn't," Vince said. "I couldn't find the key. If you'd come here tomorrow I would've been gone. I was getting ready to head to the storage unit and break in with a pair of bolt cutters and hope for the best. I figured I could put all the files in the back of my truck and spend a couple of days at a cheap motel going through them. The longer I stay away from home, the safer your mother will be."

"I'm not sure that makes you much safer though," I said, making him smile wryly. "Fortunately, I found the key at the bottom of the file cabinet."

"You did?" he asked, excitement shining in his eyes.

"I'm not sure what you have planned as far as how to clean up this mess," I said. "But Nick, Savage, and Kate all know about this."

"Then no one is safe," he said. "Angelica is no one to mess with."

"How do you know she's behind whoever tried to kill you in Miami?" I asked. "Like you said, there were a lot of players involved. Maybe someone found out you went to visit Carmen and got nervous. Remember, Angelica has nothing to lose or gain by trying to kill you. Honestly, it seemed like she was rather fond of you and Dad. But she's got immunity. Anything Dad found out about her wouldn't matter."

"It's what he found out about others," he said, nodding in agreement. "There's very few people I trust to help me with this whole thing, but I haven't been thinking straight. I've been retired too long. And I'll admit, the close calls in Miami got to me. I'd never have thought I'd have to deal with that stuff this long after I left the job."

"I've got the key in my van," I told him. "Why don't we take your car and swing by and pick it? I'm sure Rosemarie and Scarlet have had enough of the outdoors."

"You go ahead," he said. "I can't leave just yet. I told you there were very few people I trusted with this information. I contacted them and they're on the way here now. I'll explain everything and then we can all meet over at the storage shed. Call Nick and your FBI friend. We should probably have as many witnesses as possible."

I heard a car driving across boards and through the muck, and I stared at Vince in panic. What if whoever was trying to kill him in Miami had found him here? What if they'd followed me to get to Vince?

"I'm sure it's no one to worry about," Vince said. "Remember, I'm expecting friends. But just in case, why don't you go out the back and stay low."

Car doors slammed shut and Vince grabbed me by the arm and pulled me toward the door. "Watch out for the flotants," Vince said, and shoved me out the back door, closing it in my face.

I didn't know what a flotant was, and if I'd had

cell service I would've looked it up, but I figured whatever it was, I'd at least be able to see it coming for me. There was a pirogue tied to the dock and it swayed gently in the marshy green water. Gnats and other bugs hovered over the water, and other things I didn't want to think about made creaking noises off into the mossy trees.

The bayou was a cacophony of smells—hot mud, dirty dishwater, and fish, for the most part. I was going to have to add the bayou to the growing list of things that made me vomit, along with pancake batter, air freshener, and concrete after it rains.

The temperature was a lot colder on the water, and I shivered in my leather jacket, wishing I'd gone for practicality instead of style. But there was no use crying over spilled milk, and I looked really good while I shivered uncontrollably.

I wasn't sure who'd driven up, but I hoped Vince knew what he was doing.

I decided standing on a swaying dock wasn't in my best interest, and I couldn't see or hear anything from my current position. I was one of those people who had constant FOMO—fear of missing out— and I needed to see what was happening in the worst way.

My choices were limited. I tried to recall the layout of the fishing cabin. It was basically one main room that served as a bedroom and living room, a small kitchen that was no more than a sink, a microwave, and a minifridge, and a closed door I could only assume was the bathroom.

My best chance of curing my FOMO was to make my way over to the kitchen side where there were two small windows.

I leaned as far as I could without toppling into the water to see what the lay of the land looked like. There were stilts spaced evenly apart on the entire left side of the cabin, and I remembered my dad had planned to build an extra room so Phoebe and I could come with him some weekends. But since we hated bugs and fishing and gross stuff in general, that hadn't panned out the way he'd wanted.

The stilts stuck up about two feet out of the water, and if I could manage to stand on one I'd be able to look into the window.

I was feeling pretty optimistic about my chances of success. The mucky water was almost to the front of the house, but there seemed to be solid ground just on the other side of the kitchen window and up to where the river was under the bridge.

I debated whether or not to untie the pirogue and row myself to my destination, but I was afraid it'd make too much noise if I accidentally hit one of the stilts. I wasn't exactly Sir Francis Drake when it came to boats. My only other option was to jump from stilt to stilt until I reached the window. I also wasn't a circus performer, but it seemed the easier of the two options.

I heard footsteps on the porch and knew my time was limited to get into place without being seen or heard, so I took a deep breath and channeled my inner ninja warrior. The stilts were a good size, big enough I could fit both feet on them, but there wasn't extra room for forgiveness if I missed my target.

I wiped sweaty palms on my jeans, said a little prayer, and then stepped onto the first stilt, which just happened to be directly beside the dock. It was solid beneath my feet, and I let out a *whoosh* of surprise. I didn't give myself time to think or I would've chickened out. I jumped to the next one. And then the next. Until finally I stood on the one just outside the kitchen window.

I had to admit it felt good to know I still had it and that marriage and pregnancy hadn't totally stolen my mojo.

If I stood on my tiptoes I could barely see into the kitchen window. I gasped in surprise as I saw Vince staring back at me, his lips thin and his eyes narrowed. I was used to this look from men, so I gave him a thumbs-up, and he blew out a breath and went to answer the knock at the door.

Vince stood with his back to me and his weapon drawn and down at his side while he cracked the door an inch to see who was there. He opened it wider and let two men inside.

They were older, probably in their early sixties, and I could tell by looking at them they were cops. Or at least they used to be. Cops all looked the same—not in physical appearance, but there was something in the eyes that was a dead giveaway. My father had the same look.

I didn't recognize either of the men, but Vince

shifted where he stood so when they faced him they didn't have a clear shot of the kitchen window. Vince put his weapon back in the holster.

"Jimmy," Vince said, shaking the man's hand.

Jimmy was tall and lean, and he seemed to be in good shape even though he looked to be in his late fifties or early sixties. His hair was thick and silver, and his face clean shaven, showing a little dimple at the chin.

"Bruce," Vince said, reaching out to the other man. Bruce was considerably shorter than Jimmy, maybe a couple of inches taller than my own five foot eight. His hair was dark and thinning on top, but his mustache was *Super Mario Brothers* quality. He was also quite a bit thicker through the middle than his friend. They both wore khakis and loose button-down shirts that screamed retirement.

"Thanks for coming," Vince told them.

"Anything for you, Vince," Bruce said, clapping Vince on the back. "It's not like we've got anything better to do. Retirement isn't all it's cracked up to be." I raised my brows at that tidbit. Called that one right. "I've remodeled every room in our house, and Helen told me if I didn't get out of her hair she was going to put me in a home. Thirty years of marriage, and the woman wants to put me in a home."

Vince snorted out a laugh and seemed to relax some. "Could be worse. She could want you dead. Cop wives are very resourceful. Remember back when Johnny Russo kept getting those stomach aches and no one could figure out what was wrong with him? I swear his wife was poisoning him."

"Well," Bruce said. "Johnny Russo was a horse's ass. Who could blame her?"

"I heard he died in a car crash a few years ago," Vince said.

"May he rest in peace," Bruce said, giving the sign of the cross and then spitting on the floor. "Probably drunk, the worthless bastard."

"It's been too long, Vinny," Jimmy said. "It's like you disappeared after you retired. How come you don't come to none of the get-togethers with the old crew? Too good for us?"

"Nah," Vince said, hands on hips. "I just discovered there's more to life after retirement. I don't want to sit around and drink beer and talk about the good old days. I moved to Whiskey Bayou and started over. Now I get to travel and do all the things I never got a chance to do when I was on the job."

"I heard you started your new life with Charlie Holmes's wife," Bruce said, waggling his eyebrows. "How come you didn't send us invitations to the wedding? More than twenty years we worked together and you can't spare some wedding cake?"

"You were always first in line for cake," Vince said.

Bruce put his hands on his round stomach. "Yeah, but now my metabolism is shot, and Helen has me eating celery sticks and gluten-free everything."

"Doesn't seem to be working," Jimmy said.

Bruce gave a boisterous laugh. "That's 'cause she don't know about my secret stash."

"She only wants you to think that," Jimmy said. "Wives know everything."

Bruce pursed his lips. "Says the guy that's been divorced three times."

Jimmy rolled his eyes. "I've been divorced three times because wives know everything."

Vince shook his head, his smile wide. It was clear these men were his friends, and he enjoyed their company. I couldn't figure out why I was standing on a stilt in the swamp and not inside where the floor heater was going full blast.

"In this case you didn't miss out on any cake," Vince told them. "Phyllis and I got married by Elvis in one of the little chapels in Vegas. We said our vows and they gave us buffet vouchers and a bottle of champagne."

"That's the smart way to do it," Bruce said, nodding his head in agreement. "We all had a bet going that someone would snatch Phyllis up quick after Charlie died. That's one fine woman. Never did figure out why she married Charlie. She always seemed like a bit of a wild card, and Charlie was the most uptight guy I've ever known. He was always one for rules and regulations. I don't know how you stayed his partner for so long. It would have driven me to drink."

I winced at that. I'd always thought the same

thing, but it was upsetting to hear it coming from a total stranger.

"If I recall," Vince said, "everything drives you to drink. Charlie was a good cop, and he was a good partner. And I'm lucky I got a second chance with Phyllis."

"Oh, right," Jimmy said, his grin sly. "I forgot you two had a thing for a while after she and Charlie split up."

I squeaked and slapped a hand over my mouth. I didn't really remember my parents splitting up. But I do remember Vince always being a part of our lives. That nugget of information was definitely something to delve into later.

Vince shuffled his feet and changed the subject. "Who won the pot?"

"Stuart Marcel," Bruce growled. "Won three hundred lousy bucks. None of the rest of us figured you'd make a move again since you'd already ridden that merry-go-round."

"Some things are worth a second visit," Vince said. "Being a cop was some of the best years of my life, but it seems I wasn't able to leave all of it behind me. I've had some close calls recently. That's why I called you. There are very few people I can trust right now."

"You know you can trust us," Jimmy said. "Whatever you need, we're here."

"I appreciate that," Vince said, letting out a breath so deep even I could see.

"We heard through the grapevine that you

started digging into the RICO case again," Bruce said.

"If you guys have heard it through the grapevine, I can only assume everyone has," Vince said. "That would explain the sudden close calls."

"There's no honor among thieves," Jimmy said, shrugging. "The second you started sniffing around and requisitioning old informants the information made its way down the food chain. Some of those informants are still active. So yeah, I'd say everyone knows what you've been doing at this point."

"That's why I need help," Vince said. "I'm being watched, and I can't move as freely as I'd like. Someone is trying to kill me."

"Man," Bruce said, his hands moving animatedly. "This case is twenty years old. And we closed it up tight. We sent people to prison. I don't think you want to open this can of worms. We knew back then we didn't round up all of the players. If you start digging you're going to have more than a close call. And I'm not ready to go to your funeral just yet."

"I wish I could let it go," Vince said, dropping his head slightly. "But we didn't get the right guy. And I have the proof. Or at least enough to start a new investigation. And apparently that's starting to piss some people off."

"Look, man," Jimmy said. "I love you like a brother, and we all worked our tails off on that case. It is what it is, and I'm telling you to leave it alone."

I held my breath. The tone had changed and the atmosphere in the room was heavy.

"Where'd you get proof?" Bruce asked.

"Charlie always had a feeling things were off with that case," Vince said. "I never believed him. I told him to drop it, just like you just did to me. But there was something that never settled right in Charlie's gut about that case. Even after he retired he kept files and was still working the investigation on his own. I found his notes. And then I found the key."

"Key to what?" Jimmy asked, crossing his arms over his chest and leaning in slightly.

"A storage locker," Vince said. "And I hit pay dirt. I called you here because y'all worked the case with me and Charlie all those years ago, and I don't know who else to trust. I can't turn this over to the cops."

"Why not?" Bruce asked.

"Because Carmen de Salva had arms of his operation everywhere. Including the police department."

Bruce whistled. "You think the cops are dirty?" He and Jimmy shared a look.

"Somebody is," Vince said. "So will you help me?"

"Sure," Jimmy said, shrugging. "Where's this storage locker you found?"

"Whiskey Bayou," Vince told him.

"Then I guess we'd better go get it," Bruce said, squeezing Vince on the shoulder.

I saw the quick flash of steel and knew Bruce

had blocked Vince from seeing Jimmy pull his weapon.

Jimmy pistol-whipped Vince in the back of the head, and I watched in horror as my stepdad dropped like a sack of potatoes.

"He won't stay out long," Jimmy said. "He always did have a head like a rock. I've got zip ties in my trunk."

Jimmy and Bruce bent down and lifted Vince off the ground, and Jimmy threw him over his shoulder in a fireman's carry. I stayed low, but I needed to get as close as I could to the front of the house so I could at least get a license plate number.

I made my move as they were struggling to get Vince to the door, and I eyed the overgrown moss and grass a couple of feet from my stilt. I leapt without thinking, and my feet hit their target. It was short lived as the deceptive marsh gave way beneath my feet and I went down into the freezing water.

It turns out I didn't need Google after all. I figured out what a flotant was all on my own. Apparently, grass can grow like a lawn right on top of the marsh and it won't hold the weight of a grown woman. Who knew?

CHAPTER SIXTEEN

I CAME UP OUT OF THE WATER WITH A *WHOOSH*, and I slapped a hand over my mouth so I wouldn't scream. The water was freezing, and I had no idea if they'd heard me. I couldn't even think about what might be in the water with me.

"What was that?" Jimmy asked.

"Probably an alligator," Bruce answered. "They're all over the place. Especially now that the weather is warming up."

I whimpered and used the stilts to pull myself toward the front of the house, keeping everything below my nose submerged in water so they wouldn't see me.

I watched them toss Vince into the trunk of a gray Buick and slam the lid shut, and I prayed I could get out and get help before they put a bullet in him.

A branch snapped from somewhere on the other

side of the house and Jimmy whirled around and shot twice into the trees.

"Holy crap, Jimmy," Bruce said. "Could you be more of a city boy? It's damned embarrassing. Now hurry up and get in the car before the gators come for you."

I waited until they'd driven off the levy and were out of sight down the road before I sloshed myself up onto solid ground. I couldn't stop shivering and I was covered in slime and moss.

Then I heard another crack of branches coming from the area just ahead of me, and the trees and bushes started to move. Something huge and horrendous came out of the trees, and I must've hit the breaking point for what I could handle, because I went down like a ton of bricks.

"Addison," someone said.

Part of me wondered if it was God, but then I decided there was no way God would sound like Aunt Scarlet. Maybe I was in hell.

"Addison," the voice said again, and this time it was accompanied by a couple of pats on the cheek.

The cold came back in a rush and my body seized and my eyes snapped open to see two giant sets of eyes staring at me. I screamed and tried to back away, but none of my extremities were cooperating.

"She's lost her mind," Rosemarie said.

"She's a Holmes," Scarlet said. "It happens."

"What the *hell* is wrong with you people?" I screamed.

They were barely recognizable. Their clothes looked like they'd rolled in mud, and they'd smeared mud on their faces so only their eyes were visible. Moss and twigs hung from their bodies from head to toe.

"We're in camouflage," Rosemarie said, beaming. "And it worked real good too. Those fellas didn't even see us when Scarlet fell out of the tree, and you didn't recognize us. I'm thinking I should cater my wedding business more toward the hunting and fishing crowd. I could camo the whole church."

"That's a real good idea," Scarlet said. "Those people have loads of money. They spend thousands of dollars on fake ducks and bear piss. Might as well spend a little on the special day of their dreams."

"I thought y'all were staying with the van," I said.

"Well, we were going to," Scarlet said. "But that got real boring. And then Rosemarie climbed in the back to get the rest of our stuff out and the van started sinking a little more."

"How much more?" I asked.

"Just about all of it," Rosemarie said. "But I got your purse and your bag, and then I shoved anything else I saw into your purse before we started going down. It was a real close call too. Now I know how Rose and Jack felt on the *Titanic*."

"I'm sure it was similar," I said. "We've got to follow that car and get help for Vince."

"I was wondering why they put him in the trunk," Rosemarie said. "It seemed awfully fishy."

I ran over to Vince's red SUV and checked under the wheel well on the driver's side for the magnetic metal box. I found it, and it took a couple of tries before I was able to slide the box open and dump the keys into my hand.

I looked down at my clothes and over at Rosemarie and Scarlet and figured if Vince got out of this alive we were going to owe him a new car.

"Let's go," I said. "Where are the bags?"

"That's why Scarlet was up in a tree," Rosemarie said. "She put them up there for safekeeping in case the alligators got them."

"Of course she did," I said. "We need them. The key to the storage unit is in there, and that's where they're taking Vince."

"I figured you might need that," Rosemarie said, "so I stuck it someplace safe." She stuck her hand down her shirt and dug around in her bra for what seemed an eternity before coming up with the key.

"Wow," Scarlet said. "I'm amazed she found it at all. It's like its own solar system in there."

"Rosemarie," I said. "If you weren't covered in whatever you're covered in, I would kiss you."

"Maybe you should look at yourself in the mirror," she said. "'Cause your lips aren't getting near me."

I took off my leather jacket and left it on the ground and got in behind the wheel. Once we were all strapped in and the heater was on full blast, I carefully maneuvered my way out of the bayou and headed back toward town.

"I need to use someone's phone," I said. "Mine is toast."

Rosemarie handed me her phone, and then I started to panic because I wasn't sure I had anyone's phone numbers memorized. That was the point of having a cell phone. So you wouldn't have to remember all the numbers.

"You got that crazy look on your face like the kamikaze pilots during the war," Scarlet said. "Are you about to drive us off a bridge?"

"No," I said. "I just realized I don't have anyone's numbers memorized."

"Oh, you don't have to worry about that," Rosemarie said. "As your partner, I took it upon myself to have any numbers that might be pertinent over the course of an investigation. I've got everybody in there."

"Rosemarie, you are amazing," I said.

"What the hell am I?" Scarlet asked. "Chopped liver?"

"You're amazing too," I said. "Even though you're going to have to throw that Madonna wig in the trash."

"Eh, I never much liked her anyway. Except in *Evita*. But I've found Eva Perón isn't a good wig for me. Makes my head look too tiny."

I found Nick's number in the directory and dialed, keeping my fingers crossed he'd answer.

"Hey, stranger," he said.

"You know a couple of retired cops named

Jimmy and Bruce? They were out of the Savannah office. They were on the de Salva task force."

"I don't know them personally," Nick said. "Heard of them, but not much else. I think they both did their thirty and got out."

"I just saw them whack Vince on the back of the head with a gun and toss him in their trunk."

"Are you serious, or are you trying to butter me up for some bad news?" he asked.

I growled and blew out a breath of frustration. "I'm serious. Why would that butter you up?"

"I figure you'd hit me with something that sounds terrible, and then give me some news that not quite as terrible as that so it doesn't sound so bad."

It was kind of a genius idea, and I put it in my back pocket for a more appropriate time, but for now, I needed him to not think I was that devious.

"I'm serious," I said again. "They were working for Valentina de Salva, and they were on the take. I guess my dad had figured it out and was slowly compiling evidence against all the cops or other higher-ups involved and Jimmy and Bruce found out."

"Tell me where you are," Nick said. "Are you safe?"

"I'm warmer with the heater on," I said cryptically. "But we're following behind the car that has Vince in the trunk."

"We?" he asked. I could hear the strain in his voice.

"Me, Rosemarie, and Scarlet," I said.

"Of course it'd be them," he said. "Do you know where they're going? And what do you mean you're warmer with the heater on? Did you lose your clothes somewhere?"

"I'm fine," I said. "Just in need of a shower. They're headed toward Whiskey Bayou. My dad kept all of the de Salva files in a storage unit. I've got the key."

"Of course you do," he said. "I'll call the sheriff in Whiskey Bayou and hope he doesn't hang up on me. I'm on my way, but I'm about thirty minutes out. Give Savage a call and see if he can get anyone from the FBI. Do whatever you can to get a crowd. Call the news if you have to. These guys are cops. And they're dangerous."

"Right," I said. "Savage. News. Crowd. Don't die. I'm on it."

"Love you," he said and hung up.

"You call that FBI hunk of yours," Scarlet said. "I've got a friend at the news station. She owes me a big favor. We're calling in the cavalry!"

"Yippee-ki-yay mother ducker," Rosemarie said.

"Mother ducker?" Scarlet asked. "What's a mother ducker?"

"I just didn't want to expose the baby to bad language in the womb," she said. "What if she's a reprobate? What if she robs a 7-Eleven? What if she's like Harley Quinn?"

I let them argue it out and called Savage.

"What's up, Double Tap?" Savage asked.

"Very funny," I said. "I'm so glad Kate likes to share our adventures. The blabbermouth."

"It's better than television," he said. "I got that information you wanted on Carmen's visitor. I'm not sure it's who you're expecting."

"Yeah, I know," I said. "It's Vince."

"I'm so glad I'm needed," Savage said dryly.

"I found Vince and he told me," I said. "But I need some help. How's that gunshot wound? Are you up for an outing?"

"I'm still doing good to make trips to the bathroom," he said. "But tell me what you need and I'll see what I can do."

I filled him in on everything—from what I'd learned from Angelica to what Vince had told me and everything in between.

"And now we're all headed to Whiskey Bayou to the storage building," I said. "Vince is in the trunk. Angelica and Vince both said that the guy who took over for the agent in charge who was killed was someone who couldn't be trusted. Honestly, I don't know who to trust. Angelica—or Valentina de Salva, whatever you want to call her—manipulated everyone she met. All I know is she got what she wanted. But anyone else who was involved is of no use to her anymore, and she'd have no reason to protect them. But that wouldn't stop her from stirring up trouble. If she knew my dad had been working the case all these years, anyone corrupt would've been fair game. My dad dies and Vince picks up the case a few years later, and then he pokes a sleeping bear by going to visit Carmen."

"If your dad got proof that any of the FBI agents were corrupt then I can make this an FBI matter," Savage said. "I can't be there, but I know a guy who can. I keep meaning to introduce the two of you. He's taking my place in the Savannah office, and he doesn't live far from Whiskey Bayou. He's in Wilmington Island."

"That would be great," I said. "The sooner the better. And tell him not to shoot any of us. Just the bad guys. Rosemarie and Scarlet are dressed in camo, so it's kind of...startling."

"Again," Rosemarie said from next to me. "Look at yourself in the mirror."

"Good luck," Savage said and hung up.

"Why doesn't anyone ever say goodbye anymore?" I asked, handing Rosemarie her phone back.

I felt under the front seat and was relieved to find Vince had put an extra weapon under the seat, so at least we wouldn't be completely unarmed. Then I looked back at Scarlet and remembered the Uzi and brass knuckles.

"Scarlet," I said. "Are you armed?"

"That depends on whether or not you make me leave my weapons behind again," she said.

I nodded. "Good," I said. "Just checking."

CHAPTER SEVENTEEN

WHISKEY BAYOU STORAGE WASN'T IN THE MOST convenient place, which seemed unfortunate considering our current assignment.

I bypassed the main road into town and followed the two-lane S curve that would eventually lead to Tybee Island if I kept driving. It was a desolate stretch of land, marshy in most areas with big trees overtaken by kudzu. There wasn't another house or business for miles.

I pressed hard on the brakes as another curve snuck up on me, and we all jerked against our seat belts.

"Take it easy," Scarlet said. "I gotta go to the bathroom. I'm an old lady. I can't hold it like I used to."

"Look around and see if there's a jar or an empty bottle," Rosemarie said. "Men are always carrying stuff like that in their cars. They can pee anywhere. Lucky ducks."

"I once saw a man pee while he was skiing down a black diamond," Scarlet said. "It was very impressive. Doesn't work the same for women. Don't ask me how I know that."

I curled my lip in disgust and tried not to think about it, but all the potty talk made me have to go too, though I didn't think Vince would appreciate us taking a pit stop while he was being held hostage.

"This road is creepy," Rosemarie said. "This is some *Deliverance* shit right here."

Rosemarie unbuckled her seat belt, and she ducked down in her seat. It looked like I was driving around with a brown thorny shrub in the passenger seat.

"What are you doing?" I asked Rosemarie.

"This is just like the movies," she said. "We're driving into sniper territory. You think you're just driving along, peaceful as can be, and then *BOOM!* You get a bullet in your forehead and your brains are all over the back seat. I'm just taking precautions."

"I'm going to move behind you then," Scarlet said, scooting across the seat. "Seems like it'd be less of a mess."

I slowed down, not because I was afraid of snipers, but because I didn't want to accidentally drive right up on them.

The storage facility was very nice by Whiskey Bayou standards. There was an office unit and parking area in front, but since it was past closing time the lot was empty. The storage units were protected by a massive wrought-iron fence with stone pillars between the panels, and there was an intimidating arched gate at the front that said *Whiskey Bayou Storage*. I knew the gate was locked, but I hung back a couple of minutes, trying to decide the best course of action.

"Maybe they'll think we're customers coming to get something out of our unit," Rosemarie said. "What kind of stuff do people keep in storage units?"

"Cash, weapons, fake IDs..." Scarlet said. "I had a very nice facility in France once that was temperature controlled. I lived there a whole month while a group of nefarious criminals searched the countryside for me."

"How'd you eat and shower?" Rosemarie asked.

"I had a hot plate and I took a whore's bath in the lobby water fountain every night after everyone left."

"Good to know that's an option," I said under my breath.

"The gate is locked," Scarlet said. "I say you plow through and we go in guns blazing. The element of surprise is on our side, and there's nothing quite like a good shootout."

"Or I could just use the gate code and we could go in stealthily so we don't get shot," I said. "Getting shot isn't my favorite thing."

"I've never enjoyed it too much either," Scarlet said. "But the drugs aren't too bad. I enjoy morphine from time to time."

"I've never been shot," Rosemarie said. "I kind of feel left out."

"I'm not sure having hot lead pierce your skin is one of those things you should be envious of," I said.

Rosemarie didn't look convinced, but she let it go.

"How do you know what the code is?" Scarlet asked, her head sticking out between the two front seats like a golden retriever.

"It's taped to the front of the box," I said. "I guess the manager got tired of people forgetting the code."

"Doesn't seem like much reason to have that fancy gate," Scarlet said.

I typed in the code and the gate slid open soundlessly. I pulled through and then watched the gate close behind me with finality.

"Geez," Rosemarie said. "Anyone have a bad feeling?"

"I ate that lasagna on the plane," Scarlet said. "It's making me a little gassy, but I figured no one would notice because Addison smells so bad."

"I don't smell any worse than the two of you," I said. Though to be honest, I'd stopped being able to smell the moment I'd come up for air after falling in the water. I liked to think that God was protecting me.

The storage facility was laid out in an H pattern, with several long rows of metal buildings in between a single row of larger garages on each side. The sides of the H were for boats and RVs. The garage doors of the regular units were painted bright blue to match the metal roof and they were all numbered sequentially.

"Dad's unit is number 907," I said. "I'm going to leave the car parked here and creep around the side in case Vince needs help. You two stay in the car."

"What if someone is holding a gun on us?" Rosemarie said. "What do we do then?"

"Use your best judgment," I said. "But I'm sure you'll be fine. Just stay quiet." I reached under the seat and grabbed the gun and made sure it was loaded. "Remember how I told you to stay by the van earlier, but then you didn't?"

"Yeah," Rosemarie and Scarlet both said.

"Make sure you actually listen this time. These guys are not nice."

I opened the car door as quietly as I could and got out, pushing it closed behind me so it only made a soft click. I gave Scarlet and Rosemarie a final threatening glare, and then I crept around the side of the buildings until I was at the last row.

The sun was starting to go down, so it was easy to stay to the shadows. I didn't hear voices until I was almost on top of them. I peeked around the corner and saw Jimmy's gray Buick. But there was also a bright yellow Corvette parked haphazardly beside it.

Angelica leaned against the hood, movie-star perfect, wearing leather pants and a long-sleeved spandex top in yellow that showed her midriff and a giant diamond belly-button ring. She was old enough to be someone's grandma, but she sure didn't look it. I made a quick mental note to ask her about her skin-care regimen before the cops hauled her off to prison.

The trunk of the Buick was open and Jimmy and Bruce grabbed Vince from under the arms and hauled him out.

"Is he alive?" Angelica asked. She was all attitude and hair today.

"For now," Jimmy said, and then they let him fall to the ground with a force that would've hurt if Vince had been conscious.

Bruce reached into the trunk and pulled out a pair of bolt cutters, and then he snapped the lock with ease.

Angelica tossed her hair and held up a finger. "If you kill Vinny, you're gonna have the whole Savannah po-po breathing down your neck."

Oddly enough, Angelica reminded me of my mother once she was on a tirade, minus the Puerto Rican accent. But there was something universal about a woman who was displeased with a man.

"The only thing that ties us to this whole mess is this storage locker," Jimmy said. "Once it and Vince go up in flames, no one will be the wiser. Who knows, maybe Vince got drunk and passed out and accidentally set the fire himself."

Bruce and Jimmy both chuckled, and Jimmy got a gas can from the trunk. The storage unit was full of stacks of brown file boxes, each carefully labeled. My dad was a creature of habit.

Angelica *tsk*ed disapprovingly and muttered something in Spanish. "Did I teach you nothing?" she asked. "You want to get away with something, you find someone to pay. Money talks, baby. But you're a cheat scape."

Jimmy narrowed his eyes and cocked his head to the side. "You mean a cheapskate?"

She waved a hand. "Sí, whatever. My point is, the cops come looking for you. Then they come talk to me. And I don't like to talk to cops."

"You worried about yourself?" Bruce asked, calculating.

Angelica smiled, and I felt the chill all the way to the bone. "You don't have to worry about me, chacho. Angelica does what she wants. And no one will ever know I'm here."

"We know," Jimmy said.

I wasn't sure where she'd pulled the gun from in all that spandex, but there was suddenly one in her hand.

"You wanna be a snitch?" she asked. "Who's gonna believe you when we all know that a dozen people in Miami saw me eating dinner tonight with my new boy toy. It's the same people who know who you are and where you live if anything happens to me."

I watched Bruce and Jimmy trade a look that spoke volumes, but they didn't say anything.

"This is what you call cleaning up loose ends,"

Jimmy said. "We told you back when Charlie started snooping around that this could be a problem. We were going to take Charlie out then, but he up and died of a heart attack. And you said it wasn't a concern."

She shrugged. "It's not. At least not to me."

"You wouldn't be here if there wasn't something in those files that had you worried," Bruce said. "I wonder what it could be?"

Angelica crossed her arms under her manmade breasts and leaned against the Corvette.

"I'm just here to make sure you don't screw up the job like you did in Miami. Estúpido." She made a hand gesture that was understandable in all languages. "How could you miss him? Twice? It's embarrassing. But now you gotta bigger problem on your hands."

"What's that?" Jimmy asked.

"Come say hello, Addison Holmes," she called out.

My eyes widened and I froze where I stood. Surely she wasn't talking to me. How could she possibly know I was there?

"I can see your shadow," she said, answering my question. "You are like that rodent." She looked at Jimmy and Bruce for clarification, but they just looked confused. "You know the one," she said. "The big rat that sees his shadow. And then they cook him for a feast until winter ends."

"I think you mean groundhog," Bruce said. "And

no one eats him. You're getting your holidays confused."

She flicked the pesky details away. "Whatever," she said.

I hadn't noticed as the sun was setting that my shadow had shifted and was visible. I'd been too engrossed in the conversation to pay attention. Maybe she'd forgotten about me.

"Hurry, slothful cow," she said. "I do not want to be here in the dark. Too many creepy-crawlies. I'll give you to the count of three before I put a bullet in my Vinny. Uno..."

I saw Vince move slightly and I wondered if he was conscious. I had no choice but to do as she said. I put the safety on my gun and tucked it into the back of my pants. And then I stepped out from the cover of the building with my hands up.

Boy, was Nick going to be pissed.

CHAPTER EIGHTEEN

"Yikes," Angelica said, looking startled when I came out from hiding. "Have you been playing in the sewer?"

"Pretty close," I said. "I fell into the bayou."

She pressed her lips together and shook her head. "You should take better care of yourself. It's not good for baby girl. You already look like death. Where is your mama and your baby daddy? Is no one taking care of you?"

The irony of the situation was not lost on me. I'd never had a woman holding a gun on me so concerned with my life.

"I'm supposed to be retired," I said. I'd slowly walked the distance until I was standing closer to her than I was Bruce or Jimmy. Oddly enough, she made me feel more at ease than the two men did. "It hasn't worked out like I planned."

"Niña," she said, clearly exasperated. "That is because women like me and you are not meant for retirement. We are meant for adventure and excitement, however you must get it."

"Yeah," I said, slightly deflated. "You're preaching to the choir."

"I do not know what that means," she said. "But I like you. Now, where are your friends? The child in leather pants and the old lady dressed like Elton John?"

I raised my brows in surprise. Scarlet hadn't been with me when I'd met with Angelica the day before, which meant she'd been watching us.

Angelica waved the gun at Jimmy and Bruce and said, "Go find them. They're here somewhere. I want them alive."

Jimmy and Bruce shared another look, and then they skulked off to find Scarlet and Rosemarie.

"You should be careful," I told her. "I don't like the looks those guys are giving each other."

She laughed and checked her nails. "I'm very careful. Those two would sell their own mother if the price was right. Fortunately, I know what their price is."

It didn't take long for Vinny and Bruce to come back with their captives. I almost felt sorry for them. Scarlet was screeching like a banshee, and Jimmy was holding her under the arms so her feet didn't touch the ground. She was kicking him in the shins, and she'd obviously gotten a good swipe across his face because his cheek was bleeding. I stifled a smile as she swung up and whacked him in the head with her handbag. He dropped her and grabbed his head.

Bruce wasn't faring much better. He and Rose-marie were doing some bizarre wrestling dance that looked like a full nelson cha-cha.

"Dios Mio," Angelica said. "Did that swamp monster eat your friend in the leather pants?"

"That's my friend Rosemarie," I said. "She's very nice. She's just not at her best right now. She owns a wedding planning business in the Savannah historic district. You should recommend her to your friends."

"I like a good wedding," she said. "I wore red when Carmen and I got married. I never looked good in white."

There was a *whump*, *whump*, *whump* in the distance. I had no idea how far out the FBI was, or if Nick had managed to persuade the sheriff in Whiskey Bayou to stop napping long enough to come to the rescue.

I saw Vince move again out of the corner of my eye, but there was no use relying on him for help. Even if he did manage to stand on his own two feet, I had a feeling his brains were pretty scrambled.

"Let me go!" Scarlet screeched. "I'm an old lady. I fought Nazis. I'll cut out your gizzard and eat it raw. I'll put your privates in the blender. I'll make a necklace out of your teeth."

"She reminds me of my abuela," Angelica said affectionately. "I like her spunk."

"Good grief," Jimmy said. "Who is this bag of

bones? Someone should've put her out of her misery a long time ago."

"Go ahead," Scarlet said. "Torture me. You can't pull out my teeth. They already did that. I got implants. Good luck removing those suckers. Want to burn me with a hot poker? My whole body is just about numb."

"Is it weird that I want to test her and see if she's telling the truth?" Jimmy asked.

"A little," Bruce said. "But I can see the appeal."

"Now look," Rosemarie said, her dance with Bruce starting to escalate. "I've still got all my teeth, and I'm not numb anywhere. Stop all that talk about torture, Scarlet. You're a damn freak show."

"Don't mind her. She always lashes out when she's upset," Scarlet said.

Rosemarie screamed an energetic *hi-yah* and elbowed Bruce in the breadbasket, and then she brought her knee up and slammed his face into it while he was bent over gasping for breath.

"Dang," I said.

"I need more girl friends," Angelica said. "Yours are very entertaining. Where'd you get them?"

"You just pick them up from time to time," I said. "Kind of like pocket lint."

I was pretty impressed by my calm outward demeanor because I was kind of freaking out on the inside. I was trying to figure out how to keep the baby and everyone else safe, and I was coming up with a big fat nothing. We needed help, and we needed help fast.

"That's it," Bruce said, holding a hand over his nose that was gushing blood. "No more Mr. Nice Guy."

I started to scream, but Bruce found some energy out of nowhere, and before I knew it, Rosemarie was on her stomach with Bruce's knee in her back, and then he slapped handcuffs on her. I'd forgotten he'd spent thirty years as a cop, but there were obviously some skills you never lost.

"Toss me another pair of cuffs," Jimmy said. "I don't know why I can't just shoot her."

"You can't shoot an old lady," I yelled. "You'll go straight to hell."

Angelica crossed herself, and I refrained from rolling my eyes considering this whole mess started with her.

"Get those things away from me," Scarlet said, dodging Jimmy. "I've got delicate wrists. I bruise too easy. If you've got to restrain me let me get the ones from my purse. I bought myself one of those BDSM kits on the internet, and the cuffs were real good quality, and real soft too."

I think the only reason Jimmy didn't stop her from digging in her purse was because he was paralyzed at the thought of Scarlet and anything to do with BDSM. I knew what was going to happen before she did it, and I reached behind my back and grabbed my gun just as Scarlet brought her .44 out of her handbag. It fired before it left her handbag all the way.

The sound was deafening and echoed off all the

metal buildings, but what sent chills down my spine was the bloodcurdling, high-pitched scream.

It was nothing but pure chaos while I waited for the dust to settle to see who was still standing. I kept my gun pointed at Jimmy and Bruce, but watched Angelica out of my periphery. She hadn't moved a muscle. She was standing back, as if she was waiting to see what happened before she got in on the action.

"Will you shut up," Jimmy screamed at Bruce.

Bruce had dropped his gun and was hopping around on one foot. "She shot off my toes!" he yelled.

Rosemarie had flipped onto her back and was spinning around like a turtle on its shell as she tried to get to Bruce's weapon, but she finally gave up and gave it a mighty kick so it went skidding across the pavement in the opposite direction.

The kick of the gun had blown Scarlet clear back against the wall. Her lip was split and bleeding and her Madonna wig had finally heaved its last breath and was lying on the ground like a drowned rat. Her real hair stood up in a shock of white.

Jimmy moved to lift his gun.

"Drop it!" I told him. "I'll shoot."

Jimmy paused long enough to look at Angelica for backup, but she just laughed—the kind of laugh that only the truly crazy could perfect—and she slowly walked a circle around us, eyeing each of us in turn like we were rats in a cage.

I heard the *whump*, *whump*, *whump* before the sound faded again.

"I'm telling you to stop that screaming, Bruce, or I'm going to be the one to shoot you next time," Jimmy said.

He had the panicked look of a man who'd lost control of the situation and he was trying to figure out how to get it back. He was waving his gun between Scarlet and me and Angelica, keeping us all in check. Every time the gun passed over me my heart stopped.

We all froze as we heard the rev of an engine and the squeal of tires just before metal crashed against metal. There was another squeal of tires, and then an orange blur turned down our row and headed straight for us. We were all trapped between the Corvette and my mother in the General Lee.

I could see my mother clearly behind the windshield, and her eyes were wide as she caught sight of us and slammed on the brakes. The smell of burning rubber was overwhelming as the car door flung open and my mother hopped out, pumping her shotgun.

"Where's my husband, you filthy tramp?" she asked. It would've been a lot more intimidating if she hadn't been dressed for her Jazzercise class. There was something about leg warmers and shotguns that was a crime against nature.

"You would be amazed how many times I've been in this exact same situation," Angelica said, staring at my mom.

"This isn't the time for sass," my mother said. "I've had it up to my eyeballs with all the lies and conspiracies." Then she spotted Vince on the ground. I thought I saw his eyes flutter open, but he seemed to have second thoughts and closed them again so it looked like he was passed out.

Bruce whimpered again. He'd fallen to the ground and was cradling his foot while he rocked pitifully back and forth. Rosemarie still hadn't made any progress in getting up, and she'd worn herself out trying.

It was then I realized there was only one reason why my mother would have known where we were, and I glared at Rosemarie. "You texted her, didn't you?

"Don't blame her, honey," my mother said. "I made her promise to let me know the second y'all found Vince. I knew you'd be too busy seeing to the details. Why in the world are you dressed like you belong on *Swamp People*, and why does Scarlet look like Don King?"

"It's been a busy afternoon," I said. "And before anyone else does anything stupid—because believe me right now when I tell you the list of stupid is long—everyone needs to know that the police and FBI are both on the way. It's cuffs or body bags. Your choice."

"You people are crazy," Jimmy said.

"Don King?" Scarlet asked. "Did my hair fall off?" Then she looked at my mother and narrowed her eyes. "Well, at least I don't look like a cast member of *Xanadu*."

"I like your family very much," Angelica said. "It reminds me of Puerto Rico."

"I don't mean to be rude," I said. "But you seem like the kind of woman who'd have shot things up and burned it to the ground by now. What are you doing here?"

"I'm here to save Vinny, of course," she said. "I couldn't let these morons have another go at him. They might actually get lucky and kill him."

"What the hell are you talking about?" Jimmy asked. "We all agreed to tie up loose ends."

"No, you needed to tie up loose ends," Angelica said. "I needed to save Vinny."

"Vinny?" my mother asked, her eyebrows almost touching her hairline. She looked at me like I had something to do with it. "She's calling him Vinny?"

"Relax, loca," Angelica said. "I know I missed my chance for the po-po sandwich."

"I did LSD once," Scarlet said. "Nothing made sense. I feel like that now. What's a po-po sandwich?"

"I'll tell you later, Aunt Scarlet," I told her. And then I looked at Angelica. "So you're not here to kill us all? You're one of the good guys?"

She pursed her lips. I could tell that wasn't a description she was fond of. "For today," she said. "Like I said while you were eavesdropping, any loose ends belong to them. I don't care what's in those files.

I'm a free woman. But everyone else is fair game. Of course, there are too many people now who know my fake identity. I'll have to make another, or at least make examples of anyone who tries to hunt me down for revenge. I do enjoy a good revenge killing."

"It really cleanses the soul, doesn't it," Scarlet said, agreeing.

"This is how you repay loyalty?" Jimmy asked, rage darkening his face.

The *whump*, *whump*, *whump* was louder now, and I really wished they'd hurry up. It wasn't easy holding a gun up for that long. Especially since I'd skimped on the weight training and upped my donut intake ever since I found out I was pregnant.

Angelica arched a brow. "I choose where I place my loyalty. Charlie and Vinny were always good to me. They never took money from me. They just did it because it was the right thing to do." She shrugged. "It's weird, but it's a very sexy trait."

"Just a reminder that he's married," my mother called out.

"We know, loca," Angelica said, rolling her eyes, and then she looked at me. "She needs to take a pill."

"I've been telling her that for years," Scarlet said. "I kept a cyanide tablet in my locket for years."

"Could someone help me up?" Rosemarie asked. "My arms are starting to fall asleep, and all this mud is making me slide all over the place. I'm slick as a greased pig."

"You are very lucky," Angelica said to my

mother. "Vinny is very handsome and virile. He could make your old shriveled eggs sing."

"Eww," I said, scrunching my nose.

"Though he is not so sexy right now with the drool running out of his mouth," she said, looking down at Vince.

"You should see him leave his underwear on the floor," my mother said.

Angelica smiled. "My Carmen did the same," she said. "Men are the same in all cultures. Vinny told me your love story. It is muy bella. Twenty-five years is a long time."

"Oh," my mother said, flustered, and then she looked at me.

"We're going to talk about this later," I said. "Because Jimmy and Bruce mentioned you and Vince had a thing a long time ago too. What is that all about?"

"Your father and I were on a break," my mother said. "He met some dispatcher, lost his mind, and moved out for a little while. So Vince and I got close. It's no big deal. It's all in the past, and it was never something you needed to worry about."

My eyes widened. "No big deal?" I asked. "You and Vince hooked up when I was a kid? And Dad didn't kill him? And you didn't kill Dad for the dispatcher?"

"Everyone worked it all out," she said. "Eventually. And I really don't like airing our dirty laundry in front of strangers."

"They're trying to kill us," I said. "I don't think they care about your dirty laundry."

"It was a real good fight," Scarlet said, eyes bright. "Charlie socked Vince right in the nose. There was blood everywhere. I like to see a good, healthy fight. Really gets my lady juices going."

"TMI," Angelica said. "This is some *Real House-wives* shit."

"Try not to curse in front of the baby," Rose-marie said, spinning around on her back. "We don't want her to grow up to be you."

The wind started to pick up and the *whump*, *whump*, *whump* of the helicopter was louder as they approached, and I could see Jimmy realized he was out of time. His eyes widened, and he had the look of a man who had nothing to lose. That's when real panic set in. He lifted the gun, his finger already on the trigger, and before I could shoot a sliver of something shiny and silver whizzed past me.

Men in black dropped from the helicopters and fast-roped down, and everyone's attention was on them.

"I had an erotic dream that started like this once," Scarlet said.

Jimmy's gun clattered to the ground, and he held his wrist, staring at the knife sticking through his hand. One of the men in black finished the job, chopping Jimmy on the side of the neck and taking him to his knees. Another one trussed up Bruce and handcuffed him before calling in a medic.

I looked at Angelica in shock. "Where in the

world did you pull that knife from?" I asked, impressed.

"Trade secret," she said, her smile catlike.

"Everyone drop your weapons," one of the men in black said.

I saw Scarlet hesitate.

"Scarlet," I hissed. "You stick that gun back in your bag this instant or I swear I'll toss your brass knuckles and everything else I can find into the Savannah River."

Scarlet shot me the bird and gave me a dirty look, but she put the gun back in her purse. And then I heard police sirens, and Nick was running toward me amid all the chaos. I didn't know whether to cry, faint, or throw up.

"Are you okay?" he asked.

I nodded and said, "I'm going to throw up," and then I ran to Jimmy's open trunk and decorated the inside. And then I burst into tears because I was almost positive our baby was punishing me.

"Good Lord," Scarlet said. "Someone get a fire hose. Just put her out of her misery. I've never seen such a thing."

But then Nick was holding me in his arms and that was all that mattered as I held on tight.

"You scared the daylights out of me," Nick said. "You've got to stop doing that."

"I swear I don't mean to," I said, hiccupping. "It just happens."

I noticed one of the men in black walking toward us, and I shrunk into Nick automatically.

This man was dangerous, and I wanted no part of it. If Idris Elba had a more handsome younger brother with eyes the color of amber and skin like dark chocolate, than this would be the guy.

"Hellooooo, nurse," Scarlet said, sizing him up. "And what might your name be?"

If he was taken aback by her Don King hair and mud-soaked clothes, he didn't show it. "I'm Agent Hunter," he said. His voice was low and rumbly, and I pegged him for a local by the accent.

"Why yes, you are," Scarlet said.

The corner of his mouth twitched in his granite face. "Agent Savage sent me. I'm replacing him at the Savannah field office."

And then he turned to me and Nick, and I tightened my arms around Nick's neck.

"Whatever Savage told you about me," I said, "it's probably not true." And then I thought about it. "Maybe some of it is true. But it's not my fault."

His face cracked into a smile. "You must be Addison Holmes. Agent Savage has only told me the good stuff. And about how he got shot at your wedding. And something about falling out of a tree. And a window."

I pressed my lips together. "Well then, it sounds like you're all caught up."

He smiled again, and I swore I heard every woman in the vicinity sigh. Even Angelica looked like she was thinking of giving up the criminal life to walk on the good side.

Hunter stuck his hand out to Nick, and Nick grasped it in a firm shake.

"Nick Dempsey," Nick said.

"I recognize you," Hunter said. "Savage says you're a good cop."

"We're going to miss him," Nick said, and I looked at him in surprise. I was never quite sure what Nick's feelings about Savage were.

"I'm having the guys take all these boxes back to headquarters, and we'll start going through them," Hunter said. "I'll keep you updated as we go. We want full transparency on this if there are cops from any agency in those files. We're going to take down every one of them. It's a long time coming."

"Thanks," Nick said. "And good luck."

Hunter nodded and was heading back toward his team when Scarlet stopped him.

"You know," she said. "I'm twenty years older than I look." She fluttered her eyelashes and chunks of mud flaked from her eyelids.

"Oh, shut up, Scarlet," my mother said. "You haven't looked a day under ninety for the last thirty years. Let the poor man do his job. Help me get Vince back to the house. You can stay there with me tonight and let Addison get some rest."

"Thank God," I whispered against Nick's neck.

"Fifty bucks says they'll strangle each other before morning," Nick said.

"That's a sucker's bet," I said, smiling into his shirt.

"You ready to go home?" he asked. "Wherever that may be?"

"I don't care where we go as long as I can shower and brush my teeth," I said. "I'm stick-a-fork-in-me done for the rest of the weekend."

"I can make that happen," he said. "You know I love you, right?"

"Right," I said, staring deep into his eyes and think how lucky I was to call this man all mine.

"Then do you mind riding in the back of a squad car on the way to town?" he asked. "You smell really bad and I really like my truck."

My romantic bubble popped in an instant and I said, "You put your pregnant wife in the back of a squad car, I'll make sure to unknot your penis around the time this kid graduates so you can use it again."

He sighed. "Yeah, that's what I figured."

EPILOGUE

SATURDAY

Two weeks later...

There was nothing quite like waking up in a strange bed and wondering where you were.

I'd been waking up with just that feeling every morning for the past two weeks—ever since we moved back into the tiny house on Sycamore Street.

Rosemarie and Suzanne had patched things up. I wish I could've said the same for our house. There was a lot of patching left to do, though they assured us they were right on schedule and we'd be back in the house in another month. I had my doubts, but Nick didn't seem to mind simple living. He also didn't seem to mind the neighbors, and had gotten a nice kick out of the weekly NAD Squad meetings.

It was like an alien had taken over my husband. Or maybe he was just trying to be the calm one. Every relationship needed a calming influence, and

I'd found talks of renovations and neighborhood watch meetings made my blood pressure go up.

"You better get up," Nick said, sticking his head in the bedroom door. "It's our turn to host, and everyone will be here soon."

"Did you make cranberry muffins for Mrs. Rodriguez?" I asked, sneaking a peek from under the pillow.

"Yes," Nick said. "And I made extra for you so you don't eat them all before she gets here like last week."

The morning sickness had finally passed, and it was nice being able to wake up and not feel like I was living in someone else's body. I tossed back the covers and followed my nose to the kitchen.

"You're spoiling me," I said, taking the cup of tea Nick handed me. "I could get used to this."

"I'm hoping you'll remember all this good stuff when you're wishing I'm dead come delivery room time."

I grinned and grabbed a muffin hot from the tray and went to stand at the window. I was wearing flannel shorts and a soft black T-shirt that cleverly said *Namastay in my Bed*. I'd remembered to always stay fully covered from my previous time living in the house. I looked out the window and saw my next-door neighbor, Leonard Winkle—also known as Spock—staring back at me through a pair of binoculars. He waved, and I waved back, as was our custom.

I took a bite of muffin and chewed slowly as I

moved to stare out the front window. Eating didn't stop the tears from coming to my eyes. The moving van blocked Savage's driveway. We'd all said our goodbyes, but I'd been dreading this moment. It's why I'd stayed in bed so long.

I pushed the screen door open and went to stand on the front porch, and I noticed several of the other neighbors had done the same, most standing in their bathrobes or with a coffee cup in hand.

I felt Nick step up behind me and put his hand on my shoulder as the truck driver slid the back door closed and got in behind the wheel. It didn't take long for the truck to drive away, leaving the sight of Savage's empty house in its wake.

And in the driveway, standing next to his truck, was Savage. It was hard to decipher the look on his face, but I knew as exciting of an opportunity this was for him, the change would be hard.

He looked up and down the street once and gave a final wave to all the neighbors, causing them to cheer in send-off. Then he looked across the street at me and nodded. We shared good memories between us, but every season had to change eventually. And then he grinned, gave me a quick salute, and got in his Tahoe and backed out of the driveway.

The neighbors were still cheering as he left Sycamore Street for the last time.

Nick squeezed my shoulder and went inside, leaving me to my thoughts on the porch. I wasn't sure how long I stood there until I saw another car I recognized approaching.

Kate pulled behind my Audi in the driveway. The weather had warmed quite a bit over the last two weeks, but there was still a slight chill in the morning air. She had on boyfriend jeans and black-and-white-striped shirt and her hair was pulled back in a ponytail.

"And to what do I owe the pleasure on this beautiful Saturday morning?" I asked. "I thought you and Mike were going to Aruba."

"We don't leave until tomorrow," she said. "I'll bring you back a seashell necklace."

"Come on in," I told her. "We've got muffins."

"No, thanks," she said. "I don't want Mrs. Rodriguez to kill me. She's scary."

"Nick made an extra batch."

"You married a smart man," she said, grabbing a muffin.

Nick came out of the bedroom dressed in jeans and his NAD Squad T-shirt.

"I swear, I think you're enjoying this," I said.

"What's not to like?" he said. "It's the most entertaining day of my week. Beats the hell out of dead bodies."

"I guess when you put it that way," I said.

"What was that I heard about me being the smartest and most good-looking man on the planet?" he asked, kissing me on the top of the head as he went into the kitchen to pour himself and Kate a cup of coffee.

"None for me," she said. "I can't stay. I just came to drop these papers off."

"What papers?" I asked.

"Ask your smart and handsome husband," she said, putting a thick envelope down on the bar.

Nick looked nervous. And he never looked nervous. But he took the envelope and opened it up, pulling out a thick folder.

"Congratulations," he said, pushing the folder toward me.

"For what?"

"You're the proud owner of the McClean Detective Agency," Nick said.

My mouth dropped open, and I stared at Nick.

"Do you think she's breathing?" Kate asked.

"I sure hope so," he said. "That's a long time to go without taking a breath."

"Addison," Kate said, snapping her fingers in front of my face.

"Are you serious?" I asked. "This is a joke, isn't it?" I looked back and forth between them, and they were both grinning like loons.

"It's not a joke," Nick said.

I couldn't think of anything else to say.

"This is the part where you're supposed to say something," Nick said. "I can't tell what's going on by your expression. Are you mad? Annoyed? Elated? Constipated? Give me a clue."

I threw myself into Nick's arms and kissed him with everything I had. I'd never felt so loved in my whole life.

"Why? How?" I asked.

"Because you're too good at your job and you love it too much to not keep doing it," Nick said. "You shouldn't have to choose between something that brings you personal fulfillment and the baby. You'll do an amazing job as both a businesswoman and a mother. As far as how, I paid Kate a ridiculous amount of money. It was easy after that."

I couldn't keep the tears from falling, and I kissed him again.

"That's my cue to go," Kate said. "I'll see myself out."

"Thanks for believing in me," I said.

Nick chuckled. "Sweetheart, if there's one thing I've learned, it's that there's no holding you back."

"Kate was right," I said. "You are the smartest and most handsome man on the planet."

He kissed my hand and pulled me toward the bedroom, his eyes laughing. "That kind of talk will get you muffins for life."

ABOUT THE AUTHOR

Liliana Hart is a New York Times, USAToday, and Publisher's Weekly bestselling author of more than sixty titles. After starting her first novel her freshman year of college, she immediately became addicted to writing and knew she'd found what she was meant to do with her life. She has no idea why she majored in music.

Since publishing in June 2011, Liliana has sold more than six-million books. All three of her series have made multiple appearances on the New York Times list.

Liliana can almost always be found at her

computer writing, hauling five kids to various activities, or spending time with her husband. She calls Texas home.

If you enjoyed reading *this*, I would appreciate it if you would help others enjoy this book, too.

Lend it. This e-book is lending-enabled, so please, share it with a friend.

Recommend it. Please help other readers find this book by recommending it to friends, readers' groups and discussion boards.

Review it. Please tell other readers why you liked this book by reviewing. If you do write a review, please send me an email at lilianahartauthor@gmail.com, or visit me at http://www.lilianahart.com.

Connect with me online:
www.lilianahart.com
lilianahartauthor@gmail.com

facebook.com/LilianaHart
twitter.com/Liliana_Hart
instagram.com/LilianaHart
bookbub.com/authors/liliana-hart

ALSO BY LILIANA HART

Addison Holmes Mystery Series

Whiskey Rebellion

Whiskey Sour

Whiskey For Breakfast

Whiskey, You're The Devil

Whiskey on the Rocks

Whiskey Tango Foxtrot

Whiskey and Gunpowder

Whiskey Lullaby

JJ Graves Mystery Series

Dirty Little Secrets

A Dirty Shame

Dirty Rotten Scoundrel

Down and Dirty

Dirty Deeds

Dirty Laundry

Dirty Money

A Dirty Job

Dirty Devil

Playing Dirty

Gone to Dust

Say No More

ACKNOWLEDGMENTS

A special thanks to all the team of people who help get these books on the shelves. It truly takes a village.

Thanks to Dar Albert at Wicked Smart Designs for the amazing cover. Thank you to my editing team, Imogen Howsen and Ava Hodge.

And a special thanks to Scott Silverii, for reading this book as fast as I could throw chapters at him and helping me plot through the storms. You're an excellent researcher, brainstormer, sounding board, and formatter. I'm glad we're married, otherwise you'd be really expensive.

9 781951 129482